Harvest Moon Homecoming

SWEET HAVEN FARM
BOOK ONE

JESSIE GUSSMAN

Contents

Acknowledgments

Cover art by Julia Gussman
Editing by Heather Hayden
Narration by Jay Dyess
Author Services by CE Author Assistant

~

Listen to the unabridged audio for FREE performed by Jay Dyess on the Say with Jay channel on YouTube. Get early access to all of Jay's recordings and listen to Jessie's books before they're available to the general public, plus get daily Bible readings by Jay and bonus scenes by becoming a Say with Jay channel member.

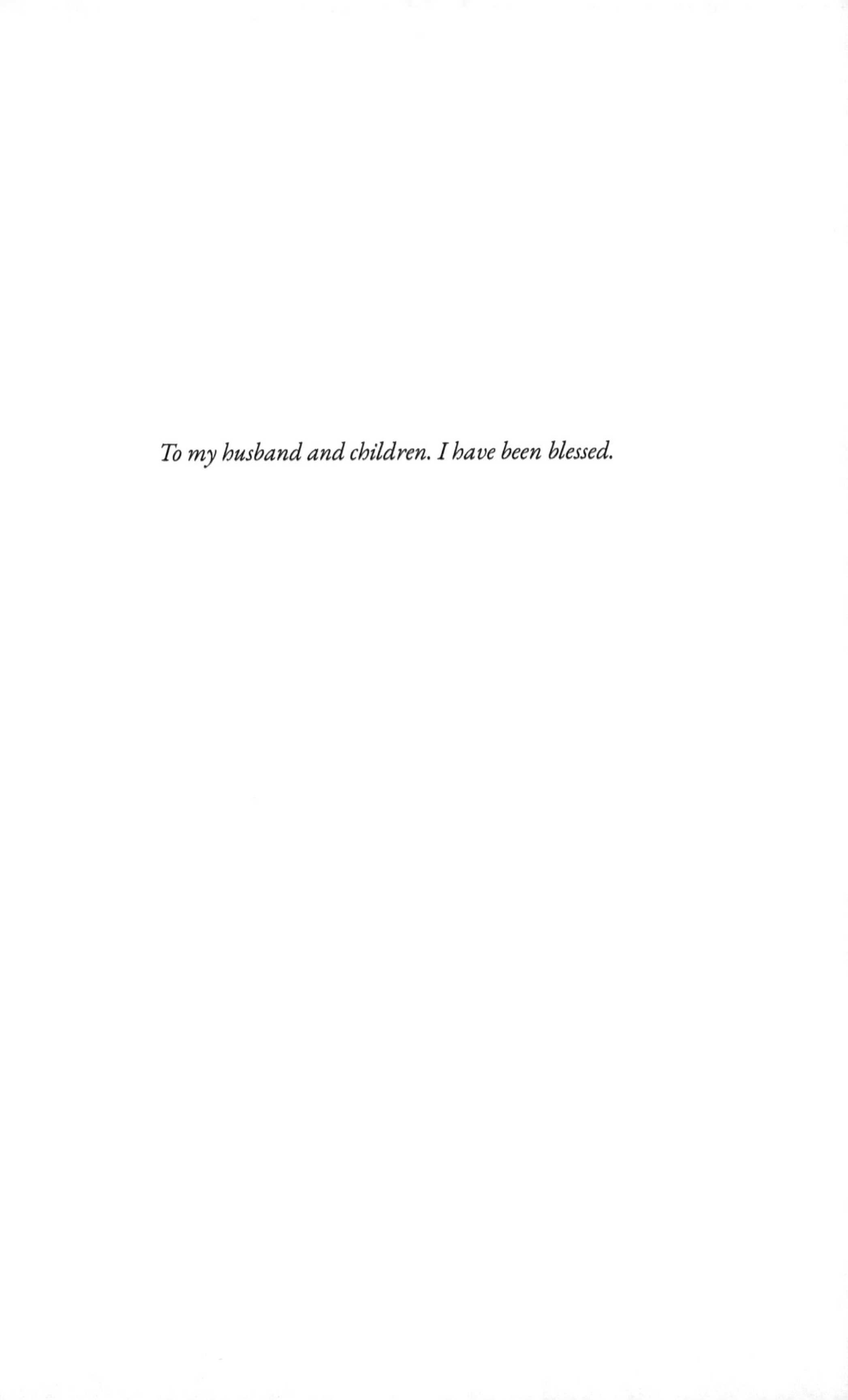

To my husband and children. I have been blessed.

Chapter One

Fink vowed to stop the chaos.

He glanced at the large Roman numeral clock on the wall of his office. With narrowed eyes, he turned back to stare out the big picture window overlooking the main entrance to the small Pennsylvania school.

Monday morning. Eight forty-three. Any minute now.

He straightened his tie, then drummed his fingers on the desk. This had gone on long enough, and he was going to put a stop to it. Today.

As if his determination had conjured it, the old blue Ford F-150 shot into view. Smoke billowed out of the tailpipe. The roar and rumble of the motor shook the window glass. No muffler. Rubber squealed and the passenger-side wheels lifted from the pavement as the truck careened around the turn. The two heads inside the cab bobbled and jerked. As the truck slowed, the cloud of smoke engulfed it. It lurched to a stop with the front passenger tire on the sidewalk.

Mr. Finkenbinder frowned and rubbed the side of his nose. He could never figure out whether Mrs. Bright parked that way on purpose, or if it was truly an accident every time.

He turned to the solid glass wall on his right. With all the privacy of a goldfish Mr. Finkenbinder would never be accused of any impropriety.

Three, two, one. Mrs. Bright barreled around the corner, her wild brown hair waving like Medusa's snakes, her hot pink pajama bottoms churning, her large orange T-shirt rippling like a flag in the wind, her Muck boots clomping against the freshly waxed floor.

"Hurry up, Harper. We're late." The frightful woman turned to her daughter, who trailed behind her, unfazed. A small pang of envy zipped through his chest. How did such a crazy, irresponsible woman have such an organized, obedient daughter? And why, in the name of all that was holy, did the nephew who had been dropped on his doorstep this fall have to be more like Mrs. Bright than her daughter?

"Crap, I forgot paper for a note." Mrs. Bright stopped and slapped her forehead.

Harper tapped her mother's shoulder and handed her the sheet she carried on top of her neatly stacked books.

"Oh, you're wonderful, Harper. Thanks," she gushed. As if Harper didn't do that every Monday morning.

Jordon Swoop raced by the window, screeched to a stop, backed up, and tapped Mr. Finkenbinder's window. "Are you lifting tonight, Mr. F?"

He gave the kid a small smile and nodded. Jordon's grades had been high enough to keep him eligible for sports since last winter, but he was still holding Mr. Finkenbinder to the deal they'd made—Mr. Finkenbinder would help him with his academics and Jordon would be his lifting partner.

Jordon gave a thumbs-up and hustled away.

Mr. Finkenbinder had lost sight of Mrs. Bright and her daughter as they entered the office, blocked by one of the nonglass walls. But when they stepped up to the counter in the office, he could again see the odd pair through the window in his door. His nostrils flared and his smile disappeared.

He reached for the intercom on his desk and depressed the button. "Mrs. Herschel?"

"Yes, Mr. Finkenbinder?"

"Once you have authorized the late excuse and administered the tardy notice, would you please send Mrs. Bright into my office?" He looked down, adjusting the single sheet of paper on his pristine desk, but out of his peripheral vision, he sensed Mrs. Bright turn and stare straight at him. His big wall clock ticked seven times before he lifted his eyes and met hers, which were a startling blue.

She spun around.

"I don't have time to meet with that pompous donkey today."

Because his door was cracked and her voice was raised, he heard her quite plainly. He could have yelled out the door to Mrs. Herschel. Some might say he should have since this was a small country school with none of the metal detectors, door locks, and ID cards that other, larger schools had acquired in the last decade. The atmosphere of the school was casual. Mr. Finkenbinder didn't do casual.

He depressed the button of the intercom again.

"Mrs. Herschel?"

"Yes, Mr. Finkenbinder?"

"If Mrs. Bright should find her schedule too full to grace me with her presence in my office"—Mr. Finkenbinder could hardly believe he'd used Mrs. Bright's name and *grace* in the same sentence, but there it was. English was a complicated language—"you may dismiss her and assign her daughter to Room One for two hours of after-school detention."

"Yes, Mr. Finkenbinder."

This time Mrs. Bright whipped around and yanked open his door. It banged against the doorstop and lurched back, smacking her in the temple. She tended to lead with her head, as if she had horns.

She swore. At him or the door. Maybe both.

He did not look up, using the pencil in his hand to make a short remark about nothing on the paper in front of him, noting the scent of fresh pine filling his office.

Ten ticks of the clock. He glanced up. "Oh, Mrs. Bright. Why, you found time in your schedule to see me after all? How nice. Do come in."

She walked in and slammed the door.

"Please sit down." He gestured toward the two metal chairs facing his desk.

"Let's not pretend we like each other, Fink," she said with saccharine sweetness as she swiped a Tootsie Roll from the container on his desk and plopped down.

Mr. Finkenbinder managed not only to withhold his growl, but to also plaster a pleasant, bland smile on his face. "I'm sorry you feel that way, Mrs. Bright." He straightened the Tootsie Roll container so it aligned properly with the corner of his desk.

She crossed her arms over her chest.

He noted the nasty red swelling on the side of her head and squelched the compassion threatening to trickle up into his heart. Any sign of weakness on his part would give a woman like this too much of an advantage.

"Since I became principal of this school last year, I have noticed that almost every morning you arrive with your daughter at least thirty minutes late. Once or twice we could allow to slide by, but your daughter is missing important instruction in her first period class. You do want what is best for your daughter, Mrs. Bright?"

"Actually, no. I was thinking about chaining her to the railroad tracks on my way home tonight, Fink."

He set the pencil down with a snap, perfectly parallel with the edge of the paper, and refrained from commenting on her striking resemblance to a fire-breathing dragon.

Mrs. Bright popped the Tootsie Roll into her mouth, threw the wrapper on his desk, and grabbed another piece of candy. Did she deliberately move the container? Only a slight bump, but his entire desk felt crooked now.

Mr. Finkenbinder clamped down on his tongue as he picked up her trash, threw it in the trash can on the other side of the desk, and straightened the candy container.

Next Wednesday, the Chestnut Hill school board would meet for their regular monthly meeting. On that evening, they would choose a new district superintendent. Mr. Finkenbinder intended that his name be chosen. If he grabbed Mrs. Bright by her Medusa hair and dragged her out of the building screaming, it would lower his chances of improving his position in this district.

"I understand that it must be difficult for you to raise your daughter after the death of your husband." Was it possible for a wife to disorganize a husband to death? "But I must insist on punctuality. Other students who are late face the consequences."

She probably chewed her Tootsie Roll with her mouth open on

purpose. Mr. Finkenbinder ignored the irritation threatening to close off his throat and focused on his speech.

"Harper is a contender to be valedictorian or salutatorian this year. Her tardiness is through no fault of her own. Because of that, I am reluctant to punish her. However, lest I be accused of playing favorites, there must be a consequence. I am prepared to apply the repercussion to the actual offender. You."

Mrs. Bright rolled her eyes. "Right, Fink. I know you have it in for me. What'd you want me to do? Sit in detention? Write an essay? Stand in the corner?"

He waited. Fifteen ticks of the clock.

Savoring the moment, containing his anticipation, he opened his mouth.

Before he could speak, Mr. Daschel, the chemistry teacher, ran past his window. His hand left a grubby mark on the glass as he grabbed it with a clunk and screech, to slow his pace enough to make the turn to the office. He still overshot. His hand disappeared, then reappeared, windmilling in the air.

Mr. Finkenbinder said to no one in particular, since Mrs. Bright and he were not exactly on casual speaking terms, "I do believe he was smoking."

"God forbid there be a cigarette in the sanctuary." She slouched in the chair and rolled her eyes.

"No. I mean, his body was smoking."

Mr. Daschel barged into the office. He stopped short when his gaze landed on Mrs. Bright.

"Uh, I'm sorry. Knock, knock." He gave a sheepish smile.

Mr. Finkenbinder did not return it.

Smoke wafted up from the man's clothing. His left eyebrow was gone. "Yes?"

"Didn't mean to interrupt, Mr. F, but the float we were making for homecoming exploded."

"Good grief." Mr. Finkenbinder stood. It was possible an evil chuckle came from Mrs. Bright, but he choose to ignore it. "Was anyone hurt?"

"No. No. You see, I thought if I combined hydroquinone and—"

"Later, Mr. Daschel. The police will be here any minute." There went his opportunity for superintendent. "And the news media. You might want to...put yourself out." Mr. Finkenbinder gestured toward the smoke. He couldn't believe the fire alarm hadn't gone off. That would make his day complete. All 328 Chestnut Hill High School students wandering around outside, wasting valuable learning time, while the volunteer fire company sprayed Mr. Daschel's jacket with fire-retardant foam. Lovely.

"Wait." Mr. Daschel glanced at his arm and seemed startled to realize he was smoking. "The float explosion happened this weekend and I forgot to tell you. I ran out of class as soon as I remembered." He swatted at his smoking arm. "But we did have a small mishap in the room just moments ago—nothing out of the ordinary. De rigueur, so to speak."

Mr. Finkenbinder blinked at the incorrect usage of *de rigueur*, but did not interrupt.

With his head lowered, Mr. Daschel shuffled his feet before he continued. "Anyway, it reminded me of the explosion this weekend, and the ruination of the homecoming float. I'm afraid the parents of the committee members have revoked permission for their children to help build it. We are floatless, and our volunteers have resigned."

Mr. Finkenbinder sat and resisted the urge to drop his head into his hands. The acrid odor of scorched material overpowered the fresh scent of pine and burned his nose.

The parade was Saturday evening.

First Mrs. Bright. Now the homecoming float. The people in this community were laid-back, but they had high expectations for the homecoming parade. Every group from the Boy Scouts to the three members of the Backyard BBQ Club would be in it.

Mr. Finkenbinder thought again of the superintendent position and squelched a sigh. He could kiss it goodbye if there was no school float in the parade.

"Well, it looks like you've got your hands full, so I'll just head on out." Mrs. Bright hopped out of her chair and scurried toward the door.

"Sit, Mrs. Bright. I'm not finished with you." He hadn't gotten to deliver the good news about the repercussions she had coming to her for her continued tardiness. That would brighten his day considerably. He smiled at the pun. "Thank you for letting me know about the explosion, Mr. Daschel." Who would have thought he'd have a casual conversation in his office with a smoking teacher about an explosion? Information his college education had not included.

"You may return to class now," he said to Mr. Daschel.

"Right. Of course." He scooted out the door, a skinny line of smoke trailing after him.

Mr. Finkenbinder made a note to have the fire detection system examined.

He waited for the door to click shut, then turned toward Mrs. Bright. Somehow a piece of her wild hair had caught on the corner of her lip. Normally, this would annoy him, but he found himself noticing how pink and plump that lip was. Glossy. Kissable.

He sucked in a breath as his heart jumped in his chest. To calm himself he reached to straighten the one paper on his desk. He did *not* think Mrs. Bright's lip was kissable. *Did not.*

Mrs. Bright sat up, looking one way, then the other. "What? What is it?"

Mr. Finkenbinder took a deep, cleansing breath. Had the smoke in the room addled his brain? "Nothing. I, uh, nothing." He slid the paper to the exact center of his desk, aghast to see his hands shaking.

One problem at a time. Or not? He had been eager to extend the appropriate repercussions to Mrs. Bright, but now he had a more practical use for her. He willed himself to remain in control.

"I believe we were in the midst of a conversation about the proper punishment for your daughter's tardiness."

"Right. My fault. My punishment. I'm on pine needles and a blowtorch just waiting to hear the verdict." She touched her tongue to the corner of her mouth.

Mr. Finkenbinder swallowed. Loudly. He focused on her eyes. "If you would like to keep your daughter, and yourself, from spending the next two weeks sitting in after-school detention for two hours each day, you may spearhead the building of the Chestnut Hill homecoming float."

Mr. Finkenbinder laced his fingers together and placed them on the desk. Now that he'd noticed her mouth, he was having a hard time looking elsewhere. The rest of Mrs. Bright might be a hot mess, but her mouth was kissable. Definitely. He suppressed his wayward musings. He was a bachelor with a nephew to raise. And a principal, hoping to become the superintendent. He most certainly would not be kissing any parents. Not now. Not ever.

Mrs. Bright stared at him with her arms crossed. She'd been speaking and he'd missed her entire tirade. Those pink lips were set in a straight line.

He cleared his throat. Easy guess that she'd just said she couldn't do the float. Actually, come to think of it, he probably didn't want her to. She couldn't be depended upon to get her progeny to school on time. What an insane idea to think she could make a float by Saturday.

"Fine. If you don't want to do the float, Harper can report to detention today after school."

"Are you deaf, Fink? I just said I'd do the dang thing." Her brows drew together.

"I'm sorry. I misunderstood." Disappointment that he wouldn't have the chance to saddle her with some nefarious consequence slid through his stomach. Still, she was certain to be late again. For now, at least he was getting the float taken care of. But, come to think of it, he'd better supervise. Drat. "Give Mrs. Herschel directions to your house. I assume that's where you're doing it?"

"Yes." She spoke without moving her lips, and her back teeth ground with small crunches.

"Great. May I presume you will not turn down help?"

Veins stood out on the side of her neck, but she shook her head.

"Then my nephew and I will be over this evening. What time do you think you will commence?"

Her boot clunked against the floor in a fast rhythm. "Eight."

"That will suit. We will be there."

She jerked her head, her wild hair flying everywhere, and stood. "Unless, of course, I contract pneumonia, malaria, and herpes in the next twelve hours. If only I could be so favored." Mrs. Bright continued to mutter under her breath as she stomped out of the room. After confirming her address with Mrs. Hershel, she strode out. She did not look through his window as she walked by.

"Mr. Finkenbinder, sir?" Mrs. Herschel's voice crackled over the small intercom speaker.

He depressed the button. "Yes?"

"You were not at the employee luncheon yesterday afternoon?"

"No, ma'am."

"I see. Well, you know Mrs. Kurtz had her Home Ec. class cater it. No one consulted me, and I'm not sure who made that decision."

Mr. Finkenbinder groaned in his soul. Mrs. Kurtz was Mr. Daschel in female form. Only her experiments were intended to be ingested. By humans.

"The elementary school principal and seven teachers have called in sick. I've exhausted our supply of substitute teachers, but each position is accounted for. Unfortunately, I still need one more chaperone and a bus driver for the field trip the third grade is taking this afternoon."

He already knew he was acting as principal for both elementary and high school today, common practice when one of them were out. How much was he expected to do? He depressed the button, thinking to instruct her to cancel the field trip. Immediately, the superintendent position came to mind. Instead he said, "That's fine. I'll do it."

Chapter Two

Ellie shuffled papers around her desk. That darn receipt was here somewhere. She had just seen it. She moved several folders bulging with papers and slid a box containing scraps of ribbon out of her way, knocking over a cup containing glass beads in the process.

"Shoot." She jumped up and her chair toppled over with a crash. She cupped her hands at the edge of the desk, stopping the flow of cascading beads, and glanced under the desk for the receipt. She grimaced. The dust bunnies had morphed into dust dragons. Any receipts that had dared fall into their territory had no doubt been consumed.

If she didn't know what the materials had cost, she wouldn't know what to charge for the wreath she had made.

The shop bell jingled and her mother-in-law walked into the small trailer that doubled as their seasonal shop and office.

"I'm back here, Mom." Ellie brushed most of the beads back into the cup and shuffled around the boxes and supplies littering the floor. The hoarders on television had nothing on her office.

"Oh, there you are, honey." Mom stopped at the doorway. "I just wanted to let you know that Dad and I are leaving for his appointment."

Ellie stopped short, automatically reaching up to steady a stack of boxes threatening to topple. "What?"

"Dad and I are leaving for his appointment." Her brows raised. "You forgot, didn't you?"

Ellie glanced at the calendar. Several papers were clipped to it, and bright sticky notes stuck to various parts, but the space for October the seventh was clearly visible. Completely blank.

"I did. I'm sorry."

"That's fine. You're busy. But we'll have to stop at the lab and get some tests done, so I doubt we'll be home before supper. You and Harper will have to handle the evening crowd by yourself."

"It's Monday. It won't be bad. Except I got hustled into doing the school float for the homecoming parade, so Harper and I will be working on that down at the shed. After eight. If you and Dad could close up?"

"Of course, dear." She waved and turned. "Oh, this wreath is absolutely stunning. I adore the burnt orange with that dark green."

"Thanks. I was just looking for the receipt for the beads so I could price it."

Mom sighed and shook her head. "You have so much talent. It's a crime for you to be holed up here on our little farm. I wish you had gone to art school like you had planned."

Getting pregnant with Harper at such a young age had shut down those plans. She and Liam had gotten married, and her main goal in life had been to be the best mom possible to Harper. Of course, when her husband had been killed in the paving accident, that goal had grown to include keeping the tree farm profitable.

They had expanded their offerings from Christmas trees to a small apple orchard, pumpkins, a corn maze, hayrides, and their newest venture this year, a haunted barn. It had been insanely popular last weekend. Which, of course, had kept her up until the wee hours of Monday morning. Drat that stiff-necked Mr. Finkenbinder. Like she had time to make a float in the middle of the busiest season of the year. If she had time, she'd have her own float in the parade.

She realized her mother-in-law still stood in the doorway, looking at her. "I'm happy here, Mom."

"I'm glad, honey. See you later." She walked out and Ellie glanced again at the calendar. She couldn't believe she hadn't written Dad's appointment down.

With all the area schools booking field trips, she needed to keep on top of things and avoid scheduling conflicts. Thankfully, nothing had been booked for this afternoon.

Her eye caught on a bright green Post-it note at the top of the calendar. She scuttled around the stacks of boxes and moved closer to read it.

Chestnut Hill 3rd grade.
October 7, 12 p.m.

CRAP. Crap. Crap. Crap. She groaned and glanced at her wrist to check the time, but her watch was missing. A casualty of her mad rush to get out the door this morning.

Okay. She could do this. Normally, they had at least two employees on hand for group bookings, but if the bus driver would drive the tractor for the hayrides, she could probably handle the rest. It was a small school—only forty or fifty students in each grade. She looked at the Post-it again. She hadn't written down any numbers. Smart. Just brilliant. If she were her own employee, she'd fire herself.

Ellie charged out of the shop door. A heavy crash sounded behind her as she pulled it shut. She'd deal with that later, whatever it was. Right now, she needed to fill the metal tubs with water for apple bobbing. Mental note—she needed apples. And hotdogs. Wait. No hotdogs. Not with third graders. Give those little darlings a sharp stick and an open fire and an ER trip was inevitable.

Had she restocked their apple supply? Maybe Mom had. Gosh, she hoped so. Did the tractor have gas? No, not gas. Diesel fuel. Holy smokes, she'd made that mistake ten years ago. Never again. The tractor was probably out, or close to it. Dad usually took care of it, but Mondays were often slow.

Ten minutes later, she had gathered glue and a few decorations for the kids who didn't want to climb on the hay bales, and filled three tubs with water. She dragged them, one at a time, across the cement floor of their main building, which was only a pole barn with bathrooms and a small stage. She'd decorated it herself with hay bales, gourds, pumpkins, and cornstalks. Indian corn hung from posts, and orange lights glittered from the ceiling.

Was one string of lights out? She twisted to get a better look. Her boot caught on the cement, throwing her to the floor, and the tub, rocketing along behind, slammed into her. It didn't tip over, but water splashed backwards, then sloshed forward, smacking her in the face and drenching her down to her boots. Half of her hair was soaked and hung in her face. She glanced down and snorted. She hadn't realized until now that she still wore her hot-pink pajama pants.

Pulling herself to her knees, she flexed her arms and legs. Nothing broken—just soaked.

"Hello? Anyone here?"

Her heart stopped. She recognized that voice. She'd just heard it this morning. No. If evolution were true, and a big bang had really created this world, please, please, please, let there be another big bang, right now, and take her out.

Nothing.

She flipped her sopping-wet hair out of her eyes. Yep, it was Fink. Quite possibly the only guest they'd ever have visit the farm in a suit and tie. He hadn't quite gotten the look of horror on his face contained. It mirrored hers, she was sure.

"I'm sorry, Fink. But if you're looking for the OCD convention, that was last week."

He blinked. Then his irritating, placating smile settled back into place. "I'm so sorry to interrupt your monthly bath, Mrs. Bright. But the shop is empty. Could you please direct me to a responsible adult so I can check in my busload of kids?"

She slapped a caricature of his smile on her face. "The bath is seasonal, Fink. And your interruption could be considered sexual harassment."

His face drained of color as his smile slipped. He stepped back.

A pang pinched her stomach. A small one. "I'm kidding. Holy cow, Fink, I'm fully clothed. Down to my boots." His color still hadn't returned, and he'd backed out the door. All she could see was the red tip of his nose. He had a strong Roman nose. A nose with character, her mom would have said.

Ugh. She shook her head. There was nothing about Fink remotely interesting to her. Even his strong nose. "Go wait in the office and I'll send someone in to take care of you." With as much dignity as she possessed, just in case he peeked back in, she pulled herself to her feet, turned on her heel and strode out the back door. Her boots squeaked with each step, and she left a dripping trail of water in her wake, but it couldn't be helped.

Once out, she sprinted across the yard to the house. Ninety seconds later she blasted back out of the house, now attired in overalls and a tee with a green flannel shirt over it. She'd put her boots back on, because her other pair took too long to lace up, and thrown her hair into a ponytail—the only way to get her hair to conform without a chair and a whip. Racing back to the modular trailer that contained the office and the shop, she hoped to sneak inside the back door of her office. Then she remembered she'd stacked last week's delivery of Christmas ribbon and bobbins and wrapping paper in front of it. Four heavy boxes. Annoyed with herself for failing to keep up with everything yet again, she slunk around to the front door. It hung open.

She set her lips and put one hand on her hip as she started up the wooden steps. Fink stood at the top, like he was afraid to enter. Grr. Irritating man.

Fine. She'd just push around him. That was when she saw the cause of the crash from earlier. The work table's leg had finally buckled. She'd been meaning to fix that wobbly leg all summer but hadn't gotten around to it—too busy trimming Christmas trees and keeping up with the apple tree spraying schedule and trying to get a jump on making decorations to sell.

Rats.

It looked like most of her wreaths were intact, but pine needles covered the floor, along with broken cornstalks, twisted grapevines, and dried flower dust. Mom had also set paper plates, plastic flatware, cups, and napkins on the table. Plus, the whole mess was dusted with hot chocolate powder from a can which now lay on its side on the floor, the lid cocked at an awkward angle against the offending table leg as though offering condolences.

Fink was stalled at the top of the steps, not because he was afraid to enter, like she had thought, but because the jumbled mess blocked his way.

"You might get a little cocoa powder on your shoes, but it'll wash off, I promise."

"This must be my day for odd conversations." Fink backed against the open door and spread his arm out. "Ladies first."

A bus full of kids was waiting. She didn't have time to dither. Or think of an appropriate set-down to his sarcasm. Ellie brushed past Fink, catching a whiff of his cologne. It smelled...good. Not what she expected.

Focus.

Picking her way across the floor, careful not to step on any of her expensive wreathes, she reached the counter with the simple, electronic cash register. Usually the receipt pad sat beside it. She moved the address stamp, a can of pens, the tray of orders, and a loose receipt. No pad, although there was a half-eaten hot dog under a few stray pieces of paper.

Fine. She'd get started and maybe it would turn up. "How were you planning to pay?"

Fink reached under his suit coat and pulled a folded check from his shirt pocket. "I have a signed check from the school, written out to Sweet Haven Farm. There are fifty-three students on the bus, plus three chaperones. Ten dollars for the students, plus a free pass for the bus driver, and half price for the chaperones. That's $540." He looked for a surface to write.

"Actually it's $545." Catching him in a mistake made her feel marginally better.

"No." That smooth, meaningless smile was pasted on his face again.

"I did the figuring aloud for you. What did you not understand?" She felt like a second grader who didn't understand borrowing.

"I heard you do the figuring. And it was wrong. It's $545."

He sighed, but his smile did not slip. Although his left eye twitched.

Ellie bit back a smile. Mr. Unruffled was ruffled. And wrong.

"Fifty-three students," she said in the same tone she had used to teach her daughter colors. "Times ten is $530. The bus driver is free, plus half price for three chaperones. That's..."

"Ah, there's where you went wrong, Mrs. Bright." Oh, she hated it when he called her that using that condescending tone. "The bus driver is also a chaperone."

She bit the inside of her cheeks. Both sides. The metallic taste of blood trickled into her mouth. She could be a gracious loser, but she didn't have to like it. "Why, Fink, it appears that you were right. An odd occurrence for you, I'm sure." It's possible she might have batted her eyes.

"As odd as you being able to find the receipt book?"

The smile fell from her face. "I use the receipt book every day. However, I am not the only person who works here. Someone else must have mislaid it." She knew, even as she said it, that it wasn't true. She was the one who had the problem losing things. Breaking things. Spilling things. Running late. Getting behind. Had to be why she couldn't stand Mr. Perfect.

She walked behind the counter. Maybe it had fallen on the floor back there.

Nothing.

What was she going to do? If it were anyone else, she'd admit her problem and tell them they could pay later or she'd stop in at the school and pick up a check. But not Fink. She couldn't allow him to get the upper hand.

She stood up behind the counter. She'd just write him a receipt on a plain piece of white—

"Is this it?" he asked, bending over in front of the counter. He straightened, holding the receipt book in his hand.

"It is." She plastered on her brightest smile, resisting the urge to lurch over the counter and grab the book.

"I believe your boot was on it."

"I believe you—never mind." She snatched it from his hand and scribbled out a Paid receipt. "I'm a little shorthanded today. Do you think your bus driver would be interested in driving the tractor for the hayrides? I would pay her for it."

Fink's lip drew back. "No. I don't believe he would."

"Um, maybe we could ask him." Ellie's eyes narrowed.

Fink shifted on his feet, staring at the ceiling behind her head. She thought he whispered, "Super," but she couldn't be sure. Finally he said, "He'll do it."

"Okaaaay." The only thing she could figure was that Fink had an odd relationship with the bus driver. She wasn't going there. She had enough to deal with.

"Right. So there's three of you, one of me. We can divide the kids up into four groups and set up four stations. Bobbing for apples, going to the pumpkin patch, the corn maze, and, of course, the hayrides. I'll show the driver where we go—it's simple—"

"You might as well tell me now."

"What?"

"I'm the bus driver."

She stared. Her eyes traveled from his suit coat to his dress pants to his black leather dress shoes. Back to his face. Bland. She laughed. "I didn't think you had a sense of humor, Fink."

He waited for her to quit laughing. "I'm not kidding."

She swallowed. "Can you drive a tractor?"

"I have a class A commercial driver's license with a passenger endorsement."

"No. You don't need a license. I'm asking can you physically do it?"

"I was born in Iowa. We drive tractors to preschool."

Ellie narrowed her eyes and tilted her head. "Did you just...joke?"

"No joke. Just facts, ma'am."

Was that a hint of a smile? Couldn't be. She picked her way back through the shop mess to the open door. "Don't call me ma'am like I'm fifteen years older than you."

"You have an eighteen-year-old daughter. It doesn't take a rocket scientist to figure out your approximate age."

That's what he thought. And she did not want to go there.

She grabbed a pair of scissors off the shelf and put them in her back pocket. "Come on, let's get these kids off the bus."

Fink followed her path through the mess. "The bus should be unloaded and the kids should be waiting in the fire-pit area."

They were. Fink was nothing if not organized. It occurred to her to offer him a change of clothes, especially after one of the other chaperones told her he'd been tapped just today to fill in after some sickness had gone around the school. But he was much taller than her father-in-law, and she'd have to cut the toes out of Dad's boots to get them to fit. Plus, she really couldn't imagine Fink in bib overalls and practical boots, anyway. Although part of her, a part she immediately shut down, thought he might look pretty good. It was the nose. Man, she was such a sucker for a strong nose. Or maybe it was the character such a nose represented.

Thoughts about his clothes made her notice how broad his shoulders were. Paired with his height and his Roman nose, well, someone—certainly not her, but someone—might think he was quite a catch. Good for them.

She ended up supervising the trips out to the pumpkin patch, which, truth be told, was always her favorite job. The vines had been killed off by frost, but the vibrant orange pumpkins, contrasted with the brilliant blue sky and brown earth, always cheered her. Orange was such a happy color.

The pumpkins were randomly scattered throughout the patch, and she loved looking for patterns. Five grouped here, eight there. No two pumpkins the same, either. Short, fat, long, and tall. Two big ones and two little ones in a group. Three big and one small in another.

She loved watching the kids run from pumpkin to pumpkin, and guessing which kid would pick which pumpkin.

What made them finally decide, *This is it*? Invariably some would go to the farthest corner—the patch was three acres—and choose one too large to carry back. She loved those overachievers. Reminded her a little of the randomness of the universe and how some people ran from person to person to person, looking for the perfect mate. What made them finally settle on someone? And those overachievers? That would be like her setting her cap for Fink. Ha.

But she'd already had a husband, and she'd chosen him like the kids who set one foot in the patch and choose the pumpkin closest to them. Liam and she had been in the same class at Chestnut Hill from kindergarten to ninth grade when she'd gotten pregnant. Liam had been a good father and an okay husband, but she wondered if she might have found something better, more exciting, if she'd wandered farther into the patch. She squelched a laugh. Maybe Liam was the one who should have gone farther in.

Well, it was over and done with. She'd already picked a pumpkin and she didn't need two. Not in this lifetime. At least she'd ended up with great in-laws. And the best daughter in the world.

As she waited for this group of kids to choose, she could see almost the entire hayride route. Not that she was watching Fink. Oh, please. But it was kind of interesting to see the buttoned-up, prosaic principal maneuvering the red tractor. She had to admit, he was proficient. He probably had been serious when he said he was from Iowa. Which made her wonder what in the world he was doing in Central Pennsylvania. Was this seriously the only place he could find a job?

A little boy tugged on her sleeve. "Hey, lady. Izzy isn't picking a pumpkin out."

She'd missed the little girl who hung at the edge of the patch, a bright pink clip stuck in her curly black hair.

Picking her way through, watching that the vines didn't trip her, she walked to Izzy. "Hey, I'm Ellie."

Izzy looked up and gave a small smile.

Ellie squatted down. "Do you want a pumpkin?"

Izzy looked out at the field, then at her feet. "I think they're too heavy." She bit her lip and watched as the other kids ran from pumpkin to pumpkin.

"Some of them are pretty heavy. But you don't have to pick a big one."

Izzy dug her toe in the dirt.

Ellie leaned in toward Izzy and whispered, "If you pick one that's too heavy, I'll carry it for you. But don't tell anyone else, or I'll end up having to carry everyone's pumpkins."

Izzy smiled, her white teeth glistening in her dark face.

Ellie straightened. "I'll hold your hand. You've got to watch these vines. They like to trip you up."

Izzy slipped her hand into Ellie's and they picked their way through the patch. As she helped Izzy find the perfect pumpkin, she couldn't help but go back to her earlier thoughts on dating and pumpkins, because she'd just realized something about herself. Izzy hadn't wanted to get a pumpkin because she'd been afraid of not being able to handle it.

Was fear the reason—the real reason—Ellie hadn't dated since Liam died? If so, what, exactly, was she afraid of?

Chapter Three

M r. Finkenbinder swung the tractor into the turnaround and eased the clutch out, allowing it to chug back onto the lane. He hadn't driven a tractor since he'd left the farm for good. He'd always enjoyed the work, but he had never cared for the stigma attached to it.

A stab of guilt flashed through his heart, like it always did when he thought of his childhood home. It was sold now and he couldn't go back. He'd made his choice. Now the only option he had was to live with it.

He half turned in the seat to make sure the children stayed seated, but so far there'd been no problems. Well, there was *one* problem. His gaze kept straying to Mrs. Bright. At the school she always seemed oddly out of place, but she looked right at home in the pumpkin patch. Laughing with the kids. And his heart had given a gentle tug in his chest when she'd knelt before little Izzy. Although he was the high school principal, he did occasional work at the elementary school, which was directly beside the high school. He knew most of the students. Izzy exuded sweetness. If he had favorites, which he most certainly did not, she would be one of them.

He forced himself to remember the chaos of the shop and office. How could anyone live and work in such an unorganized, messy environment? After seeing Mrs. Bright with Izzy, he thought maybe she wasn't the Wicked Witch of the West, but being around her for any length of time would drive him batty.

By four thirty, all four groups had spent a half an hour at each station and were gathered around the haybale pyramid. Because of its low, southern track, the sun drooped in the sky casting long shadows along the leaf-strewn yard as the children ran and played.

Mr. Finkenbinder checked his watch. It was almost time for parents to start arriving to pick up their children. He glanced over at the picnic tables where Mrs. Bright stood holding scissors, snipping bits of lace and ribbon as the children brought them to her. She smiled and laughed with the children, adjusting a piece of ribbon or sorting through the piles of odds and ends to pick a perfect piece.

He breathed deeply. Woodsmoke mixed with rich fall air, falling leaves, and the dampness of soil as it readied to spend a season resting. A comforting, cozy scent. Peace and goodwill settled into his soul.

The children were finishing up their projects, and when he glanced over again, Mrs. Bright stood idle. He found his feet taking him to her. "You have a beautiful place and a nice setup here."

She looked up, twisting a piece of ribbon in her hand. Her hair had frizzed out all over her head, and one strand was caught in her mouth again. He tore his eyes away before he started thinking about her lips.

"Thanks," she said.

He looked around. "The kids are having a great time. I mean, it could have been more educational..."

"I should have known you were coming over here to complain." A kid walked up holding out a piece of ribbon, and she snipped where he pointed.

"I'm not complaining. I complimented you."

"And I said thank you. Then you close your mouth and we part friends." She lifted a brow and stuck out her chin, barely looking before cutting another ribbon with a quick snip.

"You don't have to be such a wise guy all the time." His neck heated, and he clenched his jaw. "And maybe you ought to make sure you don't cut anyone's fingers with those scissors."

"I'm a woman, not a guy. And you don't have to be such a stick-in-the-mud." She rested her hand on her hip. At least, he assumed it was her hip, but with the shapeless coveralls, and the baggy green shirt, he couldn't even be sure she had hips. Four legs and scales, possibly.

Her face had turned red. "And if you think you can do my job better, have at it."

"I'm not a stick-in-the-mud. In case you haven't noticed, I've been driving your tractor around all afternoon. In addition, a two-year-old could do your job better than you." He stopped, realizing the tone of his voice had been climbing. He lifted his nose. "You owe me money. You said you'd pay the bus driver to drive the tractor."

"That's rude. Like I wasn't going to pay you." A little girl in pigtails held her ribbon out and Ellie practically yanked it from her and snipped it in two like she wished it was his head.

"I never said that. You're twisting everything that comes out of my mouth. I was just reminding you since you seem to forget everything else." He ended on a near-shout, matching her volume.

She took a step to him, her finger in his face. "You put hidden meaning into everything that comes out of your mouth. You walk around like you have a stick up your butt and I'm dirt. I'm just saying in plain words what you meant to say."

He met her toe to toe, gratified he could look down at her since she seemed to always have the upper hand. He put his own finger in her face and shouted right back, "I most certainly did not, but I would expect you to assume the worst."

"Why wouldn't I assume the worst when that's what you always do?" she yelled, so close he could feel the vibration from her voice.

"Maybe if you weren't such a careless parent, who can't even manage to get her child to school on time, let alone get dressed properly in the morning, I would have something positive to think about you." He leaned down until their noses almost touched, and to his astonishment, he had screamed that entire last sentence.

"Um, Mom?" Harper came into view, her book bag still slung over her shoulder, her brows drawn down.

He dropped his hand and stepped back.

Harper moved to her mother and pried her fingers from the scissors.

Mr. Finkenbinder glanced around. Fifty third graders stood in a circle around them, staring with open mouths.

"Finish your decorations and find your pumpkins, boys and girls. Make sure you check in with me before you go. Don't leave until your parents have signed you out." Mr. Finkenbinder managed to modulate his voice and put his principal mask firmly back in place, but irritation still clutched at his backbone. Irritation at that irritating woman who irritated him on purpose, and so thoroughly that he'd lost control and everyone knew he was irritated. Ugh.

"Mr. Finkenbinder?" Harper tapped him on the shoulder.

"Yes, Harper?"

"I picked up Wyatt. He texted me and said you weren't answering your phone, you weren't home and he didn't know where you were, although one of his friends had said his sister might have gone on a field trip here with you. So that's why we showed up here."

Sure enough, his nephew stood behind Harper. Towered over her, really. The kid was all arms and legs and clumsy, awkward movements. He hadn't grown into his body yet. But he'd give his sister credit, Wyatt was a sweet kid.

Mr. Finkenbinder cringed. He'd forgotten all about him.

"Humph." Mrs. Bright's smile dripped with syrupy sweetness. "I might be a horrible mother, but at least I've never forgotten my kid." Her words were no longer delivered in a shout, but she crossed her arms over her chest.

Mr. Finkenbinder wanted to wipe that smug smile right off her face. Or kiss it off. *Irrational.* His eyes widened and he spun on his heel. He grabbed his clipboard off the picnic table.

"Mother. You both lost your tempers and said unkind things." Harper crossed her arms and lifted a brow. "I'm going up to the shop. Two customers pulled in while you guys were screaming at each other. I'll take care of all that while you finish up here. Do you think you can act like adults?" She tapped her foot. Her gaze went first to one, then the other. "Think of the children."

Mr. Finkenbinder looked at the ground. He'd never lost control like that in front of his kids. And he'd been in some pretty tense situations.

Something about Mrs. Bright yanked his strings the wrong way. Hard. But he had to take responsibility for his actions.

"You are absolutely correct, Harper." He turned to Mrs. Bright and met her eyes. Eyes he'd just been inches from and couldn't help but notice were a dazzling shade of blue, ringed with black. Fascinating. He cleared his throat. "I'm sorry, Mrs. Bright. I was out of line. I was unkind and acted like a child. Please forgive me."

"A very nice apology, Mr. F." Harper turned to Mrs. Bright. "Mother?"

Mrs. Bright set her chin, looking very much like a mule refusing to haul a pack up a mountain.

Harper tilted her head. "There's only one adult in the room?"

Mrs. Bright rolled her eyes. "We're outside."

"Mother. How will I ever learn to do right if you are not a good example for me?"

Mr. Finkenbinder hid a smile. Harper was eighteen. And she was providing her own good example.

But her statement worked. "Fine. I'm sorry, Fink. You're a jerk and Mother Teresa would lose patience with your condescending BS, but I'm sorry I shouted in front of the children."

"Mother."

"I'm sorry I shouted at you."

A little girl asking for a bag for her extra ribbon distracted Mrs. Bright, and Mr. Finkenbinder turned to Wyatt. "I'm sorry. I should have texted you about my change of plans, and I didn't get your calls because I left my phone in the bus. I didn't want to lose it on the hayrides. I'll try to be more considerate in the future."

"Hey, no problem, Uncle Fink." He looked back at Harper's retreating figure. "If it's okay, I'll go help Harper with the cleanup."

Mr. Finkenbinder thought about the disaster area Wyatt's room was and figured he wouldn't be much help at cleaning anything up, but he nodded. "That's fine. I'll get you once the kids leave." Wyatt started to walk away. "Oh. Um, there was a small accident with the homecoming float..."

"Yeah, I heard it exploded." Wyatt grinned.

"Mrs. Bright is making a new one, and I told her that we'd help her. We'll eat, then we'll need to come back around eight."

"Whoa. Do you think we'll have it done by Friday?"

"I'm going to search for some easy ideas with detailed plans we can construct quickly."

"Oh, okay."

Mr. Finkenbinder rubbed his forehead as Wyatt strode away. He couldn't believe he'd forgotten all about Wyatt today. Maybe being a parent was harder than he'd thought. He'd have to try to do better. But first, he had to get through this week working with Mrs. Bright.

Chapter Four

Ellie rushed into the kitchen at seven thirty that evening. She hadn't thought that last customer would ever leave. Her back hurt, her feet hurt, and her eyes felt gritty, like she'd been up all night.

The spicy smell of apple pies baking, the homey scene of Harper sitting at the big kitchen table, her school books set out in front of her, and her mother-in-law's welcoming smile normally would have made her aches and pains slip away. Not tonight. She still had to deal with Fink.

She grabbed the peanut butter and a slice of bread.

"I put the leftovers in the fridge." Esther turned from the counter where she mixed pumpkin and spices. "I'll get it out and heat it up for you." She started to wipe her hands on her apron.

Ellie waved her back. "Don't worry about it, Mom. I'll just grab a peanut butter sandwich and an apple. I have to head back out."

"Oh, yes. Harper told me you were helping to build the school float for the parade this weekend. I wonder why they didn't start earlier? Back in my day, we spent months coming up with a theme and a design."

"That's a good question." A very good question. But she didn't want explain about the explosion and the resignation of the entire float committee right now. She had to hurry.

Harper closed her books. "I'm coming with you."

"I thought you said you had to study for a big Calculus test tomorrow?"

"I do."

"You stay here. Help Gram with her pies. When you're done studying, you can come down." She unscrewed the lid from the peanut butter and slapped some on each piece of bread.

"Harper already made the apple pies." Gram placed a gnarled hand on Harper's shoulder.

Ellie nodded. One look at her daughter's beaming face made the sacrifice of having to work with Fink almost worthwhile. Hopefully, Wyatt would come so she wasn't stuck with him alone.

"I can't wait to taste it. You can bring a couple of pieces down when they're cool enough to cut."

"I'll put that away, honey. You go on." Gram patted Ellie's back. Ellie closed her eyes and savored the motherly touch before swiping an apple and heading out.

"Thanks." With her sandwich in one hand and her apple in the other, she headed down to the shop. She really wanted to get there before Fink. It'd been a while since she'd been in the shed that served as their shop, and if she recalled correctly, the place was a little disorganized.

Ellie tossed the core of the apple before opening the door and stepping in, flipping on the light switch.

Disorganized might have been a bit of an understatement. Ellie stared at the pile of two-by-fours on the floor of the old shed, which were scattered in disarray because when she'd taken the forms for the corner posts for the barn down, she'd been in a hurry to get them put away. So she'd thrown them in here, thinking to stack them neatly later.

Well, it could be worse. They could have to buy two-by-fours. Which would mean a trip to town with the abominable Mr. Finkenbinder. That would be a fate worse than having her toenails plucked out with pliers and no anesthetic. Even if he was tall with broad shoulders and had a strong nose. That was all he had going for him.

She scratched her head, looking at the materials she had to work with.

What had possessed her to engage in a shouting match with the man this afternoon? Liam and she had seldom argued. Even though they'd been young, they'd never screamed at each other. And in front of the children. Honestly, she was ashamed of her behavior, and she planned to play it cool tonight. Mr. Finkenbinder was not going to ruffle her feathers.

Now, what should they make? The spare hay wagon was parked beside the lumber, and she'd assumed they could build something on it and pull it with the tractor. But what? She narrowed her eyes and tapped a finger on her lips.

Gravel crunched outside. A car motor died and shortly thereafter a door slammed shut. Drat. She'd hoped to be started so she could give the insufferable man a job and not have to discuss what to do. Too late.

Mr. Finkenbinder walked into the shop. "Good evening, Mrs. Bright."

Ah, so apparently he'd decided to be on his best behavior too. "Good evening, Mr. Finkenbinder. I thought Wyatt might come with you."

"He did. But I stopped at the house looking for you, and when he smelled the apple pie, his stomach overpowered his intellect."

"Just like a man."

"I'm here."

Ellie bit her tongue. Oh, how she wanted to say something about him not being like a man, but it wasn't true. Under those dress clothes, Fink was all man.

She cleared her throat. "I was just trying to figure out what to do." Waving an arm, she indicated the lumber and the wagon. "I have all this, and of course, the tractor you used today."

"Well, that's great." He lifted a brow at the mess, but didn't comment on it. He indicated the briefcase he carried. "I did some research on the internet, and I have narrowed things down to three choices." He brushed dust off a shelf before setting his briefcase down and pulling out papers and a pencil.

He'd narrowed down their choices? Really?

Ellie swallowed her irritation and leaned over as he spread the papers out, again catching a whiff of that surprisingly good, spicy scent unique to Fink. She took a deep breath. A sliver of awareness rippled through her body, pooling in her stomach. Odd.

"See this?" He pointed to the first one. A car with crepe paper stuck to it. "It would be easy, and still look nice."

"Uninspired," Ellie stated, leaning back on her heels and crossing her arms over her chest.

His mouth tightened, but he set the pencil down and drew the next picture out. A pickup with two lawn chairs for the king and queen of homecoming. Streamers flew from the antenna.

He put his finger on the picture. "I can borrow a pickup from one of the teachers—Mr. Waggoner has allowed us to use his in the past— and this one can be done in a day, too."

"Those are lawn chairs."

"Exactly. Simple. Most people don't have their summer lawn furniture put away yet. It will be effortless to find two chairs to borrow. And the dance committee doubtless has a few extra streamers they can allow us to commandeer."

"But it's ugly. There's no imagination in this at all." She picked up the pencil and tapped it against the paper.

He sighed loudly. Although he gritted his teeth, he spoke calmly. "I was looking for a simple design we can construct easily. This fits the bill."

"If the goal is to be the ugliest float at the parade, it fits the bill for sure." She gripped her hair before slapping the pencil back down on the shelf with such force the pencil broke in two. The crack reverberated through the shed. It did little to assuage her frustration.

"Mr. Waggoner would be highly offended to hear you call his truck ugly."

"It's not his truck. It's the idea of throwing a few chairs on the back and calling it a float."

He yanked the last paper out and slapped it down. "This probably won't suit your fancy either."

This one was almost identical to the last—a pickup with streamers —only there was a bench under an umbrella.

"The umbrella could be any color, and I know where we can find a bench." He cleared his throat, pasting on a semblance of his professional demeanor.

She wasn't fooled. He was cranked. Well, so be it. If she was going to do a float, she wanted it to be done right.

"If you want me to do this, it's going to be something good. Not something we slap together because it's easy and fast." She shook her head and smacked her hand next to the paper.

"If you want my help, it's going to be easy and fast."

"I don't recall asking you to help."

"If I want the thing done on time, and I do, I'm going to be here helping." He clenched his fists, and a muscle along his jaw popped in and out.

"So now I'm irresponsible?" Despite the truth in his words, her eyes widened and her voice went up a notch. How dare he? She ran a business practically by herself and because of that, she occasionally didn't get her daughter to school on time. There was no reason for Fink to be so condescending.

"Isn't that how you got selected as a volunteer to do this in the first place? By being late to school so often, I had no choice but to apply consequences?" His volume exceeded hers.

"You have no idea what it's like to be a parent, or anything else about my life. I resent your judgment." She powered toward him. Like a bulldozer. Her vision lasered in, focusing on him. The urge to touch him, to grab hold of him, almost overwhelmed her.

"Everyone else in the entire school can make it on time. You're the only one who comes in late. And you're the only who doesn't comb her hair, change out of her nightclothes, or brush her teeth." He didn't back away. Instead, he leaned down, bring them face-to-face.

His words stung. Sometimes she probably did look frightful when she rushed into the school. Another thing to work on. Still, it wasn't like she valued Fink's opinion. She gritted her teeth against the lip that wanted to tremble and swallowed to ease the pricking sensation in the back of her throat. Channeling anger and disdain to smother any hurt feelings, she gritted out, "You are despicable."

"You are irresponsible."

"And you're a judgmental jerk." She kicked the last board laying on the floor between them out of her way. Pain, sharp and strangely satisfying, shot up her leg.

"Then, since I'm such a jerk, you shouldn't want to spend any more time with me than necessary." The paper crinkled as he fisted his hand around it. He threw it toward his briefcase.

"I don't," she shouted.

"Then building something easy and fast should work for you," he shouted back.

"It doesn't." Her pulse pounded in her temple, fogging her brain with pressure. She could barely see through the red haze clouding her vision.

"You drive me crazy."

"You'd have to go a hundred miles an hour in reverse to get back to crazy."

"No. All I'd have to do is spend five more minutes with you." He stuck a finger in her face emphasizing the *you*.

"Fine. Leave. I'll do the float myself." She threw an arm out and pointed at the door as though the force of the swing alone could propel him through it. She'd rather work nonstop for the next five days than spend one more minute with him, no matter the shape of his nose.

"And it *might* be done in time for graduation." Two veins stood out on either side of his temple. He widened his stance like a football player waiting for the snap.

He didn't scare her. She hit his finger with hers, knocking it out of the way and pointing hers right at his nose. "Then do it yourself."

His chest puffed out. "I will. And Harper can spend the next two weeks in after-school detention."

She gasped. "You wouldn't." Her chest burned like a volcano about to erupt. It was all she could do to keep from grabbing him. Some of the things he'd said about her might be a little bit true, but Harper shouldn't have to suffer just because her mother couldn't hold it all together.

"Yes, I would." He jutted his chin out. She could almost see smoke coming from his nostrils.

"Harper is a perfect student."

"Yes. It's her mother that's the irresponsible slacker."

"You're an idiot."

"You're a child."

"I'll do the float myself. Get out," she screamed.

"Gladly." He knocked her finger away from his face, grabbed her shoulders, and covered her mouth with his.

Chapter Five

Ellie tensed. Her eyes popped open. Her heart stuttered to a stop, then did a flip and started beating double time.

Her chest tingled, and she buried her hands in his hair. Thick, wavy hair. Perfect.

Had she kissed a man since Liam died? She hadn't even considered dating with Harper at home. She didn't remember it feeling this good. She pushed closer.

His fingers ran down her back.

Goose bumps broke out on her skin. She closed her eyes, sliding her hands around his waist, which felt surprisingly hard under her fingertips.

He groaned and pulled her closer.

His tongue touched her lip. Like a flame touching a can of gasoline. Fireworks exploded in her brain. Bright red. Heat shot through her body, scorching through her skin. Her fingers clawed his back. Her hand slipped back to his head, gripping and pulling him closer.

He pulled her to him. She complied, allowing him to lift her, wrapping her legs around his waist. Totally lost in a passion-draped world that included only Fink and her and the combustive sensations that fused in an intoxicating riot.

"Mom?"

Startled, she pushed away.

He dropped her like forbidden fruit. Her feet tangled together and her butt hit the floor with a thunk.

Fink took two steps back. He leaned against the metal wall, his hands behind him, as though somehow proclaiming his innocence.

From her position on the dirt floor, she glanced up at Harper, whose brows reached her hairline. Wyatt stood behind her, his jaw agape, blinking slowly as though trying to get the images in front of him to return to normal.

"Um, we thought we heard shouting in here." Harper tilted her head.

"Yeah. After what happened earlier, we thought you two might need a referee and a time-out, but..."

"I think they still need a referee and a time-out. Just not in the way we thought." Harper tapped her upper lip.

"No," they both blurted out.

Ellie shot Fink a quelling glance and scrambled to her feet. "That wasn't what you thought it was. I mean, it wasn't what it looked like."

Fink cleared his throat. "We were looking at pictures and deciding on a design for the float."

"It's not that kind of parade." Harper wrinkled her nose at Fink.

"Of course not. I mean, everything is child-friendly." Ellie couldn't remember Fink ever looking less than professional, but his hair was mussed, his clothing askew, his face flushed. His gaze darted around, looking anywhere but her, and his professional poise had possibly run off with her self-control.

"My mother had her legs wrapped around your waist. I don't think that's appropriate for preschoolers."

"Maybe you guys could just do, like, chairs arranged so that people aren't sitting on each other's laps and stuff. Where I come from, if we do a movie theme or something for school, we don't usually do the love scene. Especially in a parade." Wyatt shrugged.

"Um, so did you guys come down to help?" Ellie said, changing the subject, since Fink's uninspired comments hadn't helped. Not that she'd added much. Her heart still hammered and her lips throbbed. She could taste Fink on her tongue. Intriguing, and she hadn't even begun to satisfy her curiosity. But she didn't even like him. Why had he kissed her? Why had she allowed it? And, holy cow, why had she enjoyed it so darn much?

"I have that test to study for, but I think I'd better stay." Harper started to walk farther into the shed.

"No." Ellie put her hand up. Harper was a great student and got excellent grades. She didn't want anything to jeopardize it. "We're fine." But she didn't want to be alone with Fink. "Wyatt can stay."

"I hadn't gotten a piece of apple pie yet."

No matter how desperate she was to not be alone with Fink again, a part of her heart went out to this boy with no parents. She glanced a Fink. His face had softened.

"Go ahead and get pie, Wyatt. We'll handle this," she said.

Fink avoided her gaze.

"Okaaay." Harper gave her a hard stare. "Mom, you do remember how you got me, right?"

"Of course I do."

"Well, I've always wanted a brother or sister, but I didn't expect you to leap—" She waved her hand, at a loss for words.

"—onto the first principal you see," Wyatt finished for her.

Ellie was half horrified, half temped to laugh. Wyatt might be a senior in high school, and over six feet, but he was as cute as a kindergartener with both front teeth missing.

She put her hands on her hips. "I am not taking all the blame for that."

"Mr. Finkenbinder would never do anything inappropriate."

"And I would? I'm your mother. How can you say that?"

"Mom." One side of Harper's mouth curled up in a half smile. "You do have a tendency to be impulsive..."

Ellie wanted to defend herself. But she understood what Harper was saying. Although she didn't feel like she deserved it, when one looked at Mr. Never-a-Wrong-Move Finkenbinder versus herself, she was the one most likely to be inappropriate.

Swallowing against the tightness in her throat, she said, "Go on back to the house. Study for your test. You too, Wyatt. I'm a big girl. And whether I grab the first principal I see or not, I'll face the consequences." She turned to Fink. "And if you're afraid for your virtue, you can go too. I'll have this done by Saturday morning."

"I'll stay." His face held no expression.

After one last glance, Harper said, "Come get me if you need me, Mom." She followed Wyatt out the door.

SAY SOMETHING, you coward.

But Fink's mouth wouldn't open. He hadn't been able to come forward to defend Mrs. Bright thirty seconds ago, and he couldn't think of anything to say after the door closed behind Harper and Wyatt.

He had kissed Mrs. Bright.

His fingers itched to reach for her. He shoved his hands in his pockets.

The kiss. It had been...phenomenal. Earthshaking. All-encompassing. He hadn't wanted it to end. Not ever—what was wrong with him?

He couldn't have actually enjoyed kissing Mrs. Bright.

Heck, yeah. He had.

He wanted to do it again. Part of him was disgusted by that thought. Another part wanted more, maybe wanted to see how far her *bad* reputation would take her.

With him? Not far, he'd wager.

But all he had to do was remind himself of the superintendent position. The prestige he'd always wanted. The academic jewel. Quite an accomplishment, especially as young as he was. He'd worked too hard, and he wanted—no, needed—the vindication. He could, and would, control himself.

Shaking his head, Fink made sure his face showed nothing of his inner turmoil as Ell...er, Mrs. Bright, paced beside the wagon.

"So...the theme for homecoming is Harvest Moon. We ought to have a big moon, maybe somehow shine a light, and maybe have cardboard cutouts of a boy and a girl that could cast a romantic shadow on the moon." Mrs. Bright stood with arms akimbo in front of the old wagon. Keeping her eyes on it, she walked along, as though picturing it all in her imagination. "Then, of course, I can provide the usual fall decorations, and since the parade is the National Farmers' Day Parade, we should also have a tribute to farmers. And we should definitely have scaffolding, to have the king and queen up off the floor of the wagon, where everyone can see them—they could do the shadows on the moon. No, that won't work, because they need to wave. And toss candy."

Mrs. Bright continued rattling on. Fine. She was going to ignore the kiss. And the argument. That was fine. He'd keep his mouth shut and help her so they could get this thing done by Saturday.

He let her talk and plan. When she started grabbing two-by-fours, he helped her carry them. When she picked up the bag of tools, he carried it to the bench for her. For over three hours he carried and sawed, hammered and screwed. Their conversation was minimal. *Pass the hammer. Measure thirty-six inches.*

He hated working with no plan, but he wasn't going to risk another argument. No, he'd love to have another argument—he couldn't see any rhyme or reason to what she was doing, and he didn't think the base of the structure had the proper support to hold any kind of weight—but he wasn't going to risk another *kiss*. So he kept his mouth shut. He could hardly put his tongue in her delectable mouth if he had his teeth clamped tight in front of it.

She had amazing eyes, plump, beautiful lips, and a sweet mouth, but he wasn't going to fall for any of that. No, sir. He'd build this float and get the heck out.

At one a.m., she stopped. "I can't believe it's that late," she said after asking him the time. "I can't believe the kids haven't been back down."

"Wyatt texted me two hours ago. Said your father-in-law was taking him home."

"Oh. Harper probably went to bed, then."

"It is a school night." He refrained from saying most parents would have insisted their children be in bed long before this.

"Well, I wanted to have the frame done so we could finish it up tomorrow."

"Hmm."

"I just want to put one more board up there." She pointed to a corner.

"I'm not sure how sturdy it is," Fink said.

Mrs. Bright rolled her eyes. "Seriously, Fink. You're such a downer. This thing would give the Brooklyn Bridge a run for its money." To prove her point, she grabbed a two-by-four and yanked back and forth on it. The wagon rocked forward and the structure swayed. She let go, but it was too late.

"Watch out!" Mr. Finkenbinder grabbed Mrs. Bright and dove into the far corner of the barn as the structure he'd spent the last five hours building came crashing down.

Chapter Six

Dust flew. The wagon lurched. Mr. Finkenbinder didn't look back, but kept Mrs. Bright covered, in case a stray board fell this way.

The crashing and bumping stopped, and quietness filled the shed.

Mrs. Bright, stretched out under him, seemed to slump into the floor after she peeked over his shoulder at the mess scattered around the wagon. She closed her eyes and lay her head back.

"This must be where I say you were right," she whispered.

Something stirred in his chest. He'd seen her hassled. He'd seen her harried. Angry. Defiant. Smug. Tired. Determined. But he'd never seen her defeated.

"Hey." He grabbed her chin and gave it a shake. When she opened her eyes, he put his face in front of hers. "We'll get this. Now we know what doesn't work."

She snorted. "No. It's hopeless. This was too big of a project for us." She looked away, and he nudged her chin again, but she ignored him. "There's a bunch of mangled up two-by-fours beside us, and it's all my fault. You can say it. I know you're dying to." She bit her lip.

"I'm dying to say…" He was dying to say she had spectacular blue eyes. Kissable lips. A mouth sweeter than any he had ever imagined. "I'm dying to say I loved your idea of the big, full moon with silhouettes on it. And we can do it." He focused on her forehead. "But not tonight. Right now, we're going to take that thing apart, salvage what we can of the boards, and then call it a night."

She sighed and shut her eyes. Her body moved slightly under his. He closed his eyes. When had Ellie, er, Mrs. Bright, become a temptation?

~

ELLIE HAD PLANNED to be on time Tuesday morning. She really had. But school had been in session for at least a half an hour before her truck careened around the turn and into the parking lot.

Drat Bubba down at Dick's garage. He'd charged her full price for a brake job that only worked half the time. Or possibly the old jalopy's brake lines had sprung another leak. Whatever. She definitely needed Bubba to bump her next appointment to the top of the waiting list so she wouldn't have to park on the sidewalk where it dipped and cracked in order to keep her truck from rolling and hitting anyone since the emergency brake didn't work either.

She hadn't had time to ream him out about it, since it'd been almost three this morning before she and Fink had gotten everything taken apart. They'd have been done a heck of a lot sooner, except Fink had insisted on stacking everything neatly, organizing it in rows according to length, putting the reusable nails and screws back in the bin and throwing the rest away. More than once, she'd picked up a board, at his command, and carried it to its proper pile while repressing the urge to remove his internal organs and line them up into neat little rows too.

But that was then, and at least she'd learned this about herself: even when provoked, with easy access to sharp tools, she was unlikely to commit coldblooded murder. Much as she desperately wanted to kill him, not *kiss* him, of course.

Because after she'd gone to bed, she'd felt his kiss when she had closed her eyes. And his surprisingly hard abs, soft lips, and gentle hands.

It had been hard to roll out of bed this morning.

As she ripped into the parking lot, she spotted a man getting out of his four-door sedan. A sleek, expensive-looking model. A boy, looking a lot like Wyatt, got out of the passenger side. The man, briefcase in hand, wearing dress shirt and tie, but no suit coat, power-walked toward the sidewalk. The boy ran.

"Mom." Harper's voice shook from the wrenching of the pickup. "That's Mr. F and Wyatt."

"Fink is late?" She did a double take. "Fink isn't wearing a suit coat?" What was the world coming to? She'd never seen that man at school in less than a full-out suit. Buttoned up to his chin.

"Looks like it."

"Later than us?" Ellie couldn't believe it. She hopped out of the truck and rushed around the front, her boots clomping. Fink reached the door just before her. He yanked it open, then stood, holding it for Harper, then her.

"Good morning, Fink," Ellie said as she swished past him, pleased she'd taken the time to throw on jeans and a flannel shirt. Her hair, well, she'd work on that tomorrow.

"Good morning, Elli...er...Mrs. Bright. Harper."

Wyatt had gone ahead of his uncle, and now held the second of the pair of doors. Ellie greeted him as she swept past.

She pulled the blank paper out of her pocket. "Do you have a pen, Harper?"

"Just a pen?"

Ellie looked back, waving the paper.

"Wow, Mom. You're organized this morning." Harper placed a pen in Ellie's outstretched hand.

Ellie looked back, intending to smile at her daughter. But Fink's gaze captured hers.

He didn't yell at her for being late. Rather, he smiled. And, drat her crazy heart. It flipped like a performer on a trapeze. That was when she noticed something else about Fink: he had straight, white teeth.

Darn it to the pea patch and back. She was a sucker for good teeth.

~

Mr. Finkenbinder walked into the shop at a quarter 'til eight. He'd wanted to start earlier so he wasn't late for school again, but Mrs. Bright couldn't leave until closing time. Which turned out well since he was able to meet with Jordon to help with his Trig homework.

Mrs. Bright stood beside the wagon, staring at it with her head tilted. She glanced at him and waved when he walked in.

"Good evening, Mrs. Bright." They were not going to fight tonight if he could help it.

She looked back at the wagon and crossed her arms over her chest. "We tried it my way yesterday, and that didn't work. So tonight I figured we'd do it your way. Only I was hoping we could use the wagon and tractor rather than a pickup."

"Hmm."

She glanced his way again. "Is Wyatt with you?"

"He's at your house and going to come down when Harper's pies come out of the oven."

Mrs. Bright snorted. "Well, I think we'll really need them tonight. I have everything we need to decorate this in a traditional way, but most of it is still out in the field—we didn't carry in anything we didn't need for the shop. Thankfully there hasn't been a hard frost yet this year, so all we have to do is go get it. Except the hay bales. They're in the barn."

Fink walked to where she stood. Did she stiffen beside him? Was she afraid he was going to grab her and kiss her again? Maybe he should apologize. But he couldn't. He wasn't sorry.

Holding up his briefcase, he said, "I brought a couple of pictures."

Her brows furrowed. "Huh?"

After brushing off the back of the wagon, he set his briefcase down. The clasps clicked as he opened them and pulled out some papers. The finished design was on top. He held it up. "This is the closest I could come to what you described last night."

Ellie gasped. She covered her mouth with her hand and leaned closer to the paper. Her eyes lit up. They searched the page, looking for flaws, probably. "It's perfect," she said. "Exactly what I was talking about."

Fink allowed himself a small smile. A thrill shot down his spine. Victory. No. Actually the look on Ellie's face was what caused his thrill. Half wonder, half admiration. It made him want to do something to cause that look again. To have those amazing blue eyes settle warmly upon him. And, heaven help him, this morning she'd worn jeans to school rather than her normal sleepwear. *Hotdog with anchovies.* Ellie had a nice, well-rounded little tush. Very nice.

He swallowed. *Focus.*

"But I don't want to do it."

"What?" he asked. "Why?"

"It's too much. You were right yesterday. I wanted to do something nice. Something better than anyone else. The best float ever. But you can't start at the last minute, whacking something together slipshod, and expect it to turn out. You need a plan. And you need enough time to accomplish it." Her lips turned down, and she looked at the wagon where her framework had disintegrated. "This needs to be done by Saturday. I think we could spend the time and do something a little nicer, but this is important to you, so let's get it done."

She was giving up the design she wanted for his peace of mind?

He laid the paper back down inside his briefcase and cleared his throat. "Thank you." He paused. "I did think that since you are helping, if you want to put a banner or some kind of advertisement for the farm on the float or tractor, that would be fine."

Her brows shot up. "Wow. If it won't ruin the look of the float, I might do that. I've been trying to increase business enough to make it finically feasible to hire someone to help so I can spend more time making decorations. I certainly won't turn down a little free advertising for the farm."

"Well, it is the school float and we can't do anything big or gaudy."

"I know that," she snapped.

"Of course you do," he snapped back. "Just like you know what time to get up in the morning."

"Are you incapable of allowing the past to rest?"

"That was today." He was actually tempted to roll his eyes.

"You were late too."

"You rubbed off on me."

"Stop acting like I'm stupid." She crossed her arms and stomped her foot.

"I can hear you just fine. You don't need to screech. I was only saying I want to make sure the school comes first." He tried to keep his voice under control.

"I wasn't trying to overshadow the school." She stepped toward him.

"Just making sure." He didn't back down. They stood toe to toe.

"If you didn't want me to put the farm name on the float, why did you offer it?"

"Why do you always get upset with everything I say?"

She rolled her eyes. "I don't. You're the one who got upset first."

"It was you. I want the farm on it." He planted his feet. He would not back away from her. Drat this stubborn woman.

"You're not acting like it."

"I wouldn't have offered if I didn't." His neck was hot and he couldn't keep his voice from matching her volume. Exceeding it.

"Just forget about it. Keep the farm out of it."

"I said the farm could go on." He enunciated each word clearly. And loudly.

"You didn't mean it," she shouted. Bright red spots lit both her cheeks.

"I meant it," he shouted back.

They stood with their faces inches apart, panting. Her breath was hot, but sweet on his lips. Her eyes shone. She was, quite possibly, the most alive woman he'd ever met. Or maybe she just made him feel alive. Because he did. His heart was thumping, his entire body tingled, and, although irritation bunched in his chest, something else, something bigger than his body could contain, made him want to float up or expand. Like joy that bubbled in his soul. Only he was face-to-face, toe-to-toe, and shouting at the woman in front of him. He should be angry. And maybe he was a little, but that wasn't the emotion driving him right now.

His eyes widened. He knew what it was. *Passion*.

Which was why he shouldn't have been surprised when Ellie stood on tiptoe, leaned in, grabbed his neck, and covered his mouth with hers. Shouldn't have been. But was.

But his body wasn't. His arms swathed around her, pulling her close. He pressed into her, her back against the hay wagon, her hands shoved in his hair, her lips moving under his. His hand touched the smooth, warm material on her back, traced the curve of her spine. She shivered, and bright orange lights exploded behind his closed eyelids.

A little moan escaped her lips and she pulled him even closer. She was so sweet, so *alive* in his arms. The hand on her back slid up, fitting to the side of her rib cage, moving up...

Chapter Seven

"Uncle Fink?"

"Mom?"

He broke the kiss, but this time he didn't drop her like she was on fire. He was the one on fire. He rested his forehead against hers, trying to regain a semblance of normalcy. "We should have expected that, right?" he whispered.

"The kiss or the interruption?" She laughed. Shakily. Her hands fell from his shoulders to his waist, but stayed there like she couldn't quite let go. Or maybe needed the support. He certainly did. But her face was upturned, her blue eyes sparkled into his. He could get used to being around a woman with so much vivacity.

"Both?" He slid his hands out from under her shirt. Reluctantly. Her eyelids slid closed, and it was all he could do not to pull her back to him. But he forced himself to step away.

"I suppose you two were discussing float ideas again?" Harper asked with not a little sarcasm.

"From the house it sounded like they were killing each other. But we walk in and it looks like they'll be announcing wedding plans." Wyatt shrugged.

Fink's eyes widened, and he turned. Was she as shocked at that statement as he?

Her face had gone white and she wouldn't meet his eyes.

Yeah, that's what he thought. The kissing was a fluke. Ellie and he were not relationship material. How could people who were such polar opposites get along in a romantic relationship? Every time they were together, they fought like cats over a clothesline.

Ellie pushed herself away from the wagon. She tugged the bottom of her shirt down. Fink's hand was halfway to her to help before he realized it. He ran it through his hair instead and turned around.

Remembering the float, he asked, "So, um, Mrs. Bright, what do you want us to carry in for you?"

She moved away from him, to the back of the wagon, and looked at it. "I'd say we need at least ten bales of hay. Those are in the barn. Maybe fifty stalks of corn." She looked at Harper. "Is there any of that pretty Green Dent indian corn left?"

"I can check."

"If we have any, bring ten ears or so. And some of the regular indian corn."

Fink reached around her for his briefcase. She was rattling this stuff off, and he couldn't shake the need to make a list. He took out a notepad and pen.

She slid sideways and crossed her arms over her chest as though in self-defense, and he couldn't blame her. He breathed in the scent of pine and passion that he would forever associate with her.

He tapped his pen on the paper. "So, ten bales of hay, fifty stalks of corn, ten ears of green indian corn, and some regular indian corn. Anything else?"

"I'll get string and scissors," Ellie said.

He jotted those down too.

"Also, we'll carry pumpkins and gourds from the fields. The gourds can go in a bushel basket, with two people carrying it between them. That's a lot more efficient than trying to make a hundred trips, dropping them the whole way."

"Wyatt and I will get the corn and we'll use the four-wheeler for the hay bales. If you two can keep from fighting—"

"And kissing," Wyatt added.

"If your uncle can keep his hands off me." Ellie threw the words over her shoulder as she moved the hammer and nails out of the way.

He paused, his pen in midair. "If you can keep from throwing yourself at me."

"I most certainly did no such thing."

"If I hadn't caught you, you'd have drilled your nose into the floor."

"Of all the arrogant, no-good, nasty things—"

"Mother." Harper sounded like the parent.

She must have the patience of a saint to live with that woman. Fink put his list and pen into his briefcase and set it on a shelf.

Harper handed Ellie the bushel basket. "Can you and Mr. F get the gourds and pumpkins?"

"If he can keep his mouth shut, it won't be a problem," Ellie mumbled. "Turn on the floodlights when you go out, please," she said to Harper as Harper disappeared out the door.

Fink reached for the basket. "I'll carry it."

"Fine."

"Ellie..." He placed a hand gently on her arm. She stopped but kept her head bowed. "Could we maybe...be friends?"

She swallowed.

He shuffled his feet and resisted the urge to rub her arm. His palm heated and little tingles ran up his arm while he waited, breathless, for her to speak. Why was her answer so important to him?

Looking up, she gave him a little smile and nodded. He smiled back, wanting to step forward and...what? Kiss her again?

Friends, Fink.

Instead he said, "Come on. Show me where the great gourd patch is."

She laughed. "It's not far. I promise."

ELLIE ADJUSTED the twine on the cornstalks and reached for the scissors. They were exactly where they were supposed to be. She hadn't set them there. On a normal day, when she worked alone, nothing was ever where it belonged. She'd spend more time looking for the dang things than actually using them.

Not today.

She snipped the twine, then stopped and looked around. The gourds were organized by size and shape, the pumpkins arranged neatly on the floor. Fink had zero artistic abilities. She half suspected he might even be colorblind, but he was unequaled as a project manager.

She tossed the scissors aside, like she normally would, to test a new hypothesis that had just dawned in her brain. Casually she said, "A girl could get used to this."

"Huh?" Fink looked up from the notebook he was writing in.

"Nothing. What are you writing now?"

"Just keeping track of how much of your stuff goes on the wagon. I want to make sure we pay you for everything." He set the notebook aside and moved the scissors and twine to the edge of the wagon. Just like she thought he would. She grinned. He didn't notice since he looked back at the notebook and made another mark in it. She might have done most of the hands-on work, but Fink had been the wind that had allowed her kite to fly.

"You don't need to. It's our school too." After twisting the twine tight, she tied a knot, then stepped back to check out her handiwork.

"I can't pay you for the time, but there's still some money in the budget for the float. You should get something out of this."

"Hand me that one, please." She pointed to a large pumpkin on the floor about the same size as the one she'd placed on the opposite side of the wagon.

After handing it up, he went back and closed the gap removing it had left. "It's looking pretty good."

"I think we're almost finished." It was hard to believe she could almost say she enjoyed working with Fink.

But not as much as she enjoyed kissing him.

Warmth spread through her chest at the thought. Her cheeks heated and she directed her attention to the wagon display.

Hay bales, cornstalks, pumpkins, and gourds, arranged artistically but nothing spectacular. They certainly wouldn't be winning first prize for best float. She tamped down her irritation. Not putting her best effort into making a super great, creative float gave her a nasty feeling in the pit of her stomach. Like she was being lazy or sloppy. She didn't like to see those qualities in herself. Maybe it was the inferiority complex she had from never getting her diploma, but she always pushed herself to excel in everything she did. A school float was no different. Plus, art was her passion. If she had the time, she could make a spectacular float.

But obviously the right decision was to bow to Fink's desire to get it done quickly. Although a part of her wished they weren't finished. She didn't mind—no, she actually enjoyed—spending time with Fink. Shockingly, she was disappointed there would be no need to see him tomorrow night.

He stood back, arms planted on his hips. "Hop down and look at it from back here."

She jumped down and walked toward him.

He checked his watch. "Wow. Two a.m. Where does the time go?"

"Glad we sent the kids up. What time was that? Eleven?"

"Something like that." He waved his arm at the decked-out wagon. "This is amazing. I have no idea how you took string and vegetables and turned them into something so beautiful." His voice lowered and he smiled tenderly. "That takes talent."

She shrugged, ignoring the warmth in her chest. She almost felt like he was admiring her instead of her work. "Lots of people can do stuff like that. It's no big deal."

"It's a big deal to people who can't."

"Thanks for your help." The uncomfortable sense that he had begun to see her as someone of worth rather than the woman perpetually late for school unsettled her stomach. She wasn't sure she wanted Fink to notice her at all. Instinctively, she knew that way lay heartache. For her. Plus, someone like Fink wasn't supposed to notice someone like her. "I didn't have to search for my scissors once. Which is unprecedented for sure."

"Organization is one of my talents." He smiled, handsome in a way a school principal had no right being, and her heart thumped. The smile lit his face up, his square jaw flexed, and his eyes crinkled. "I think we worked pretty well together. I supposed there's a reason opposites attract."

Her face froze.

His eyes widened.

Had he just admitted to being attracted to her?

Seconds ticked by as they stared at each other.

"So..."

"Yeah..."

Ellie shook her head and walked back to the wagon to gather her twine and scissors.

Fink cleared his throat. "Um, do you want these extra gourds and pumpkins carried back out?"

"No. They're fine." She walked to the door, then paused to wait for him to grab his briefcase and walk between the neatly piled gourds and the line of pumpkins. She stuck out her hand.

His brows lifted.

"Thanks. It really was a pleasure...surprisingly...to work with you." She tilted her head and grinned. Man, she couldn't believe she was actually going to miss him.

He shook her hand firmly. "It was an honor to work with you as well." His hand squeezed hers before he dropped it. "I have the list of materials we used. You get me prices, and I'll make sure the farm gets a check."

She flipped the lights off, and he shut the door behind them. For one small moment, she wondered what it would be like to walk home with this man every night. To have the companionship of someone who bolstered her weaknesses. To share kisses like the one they had earlier. She'd never experienced passion that explosive.

She sighed into the crisp fall darkness. Fink was pretty serious. An academic. He wouldn't be interested in someone like her. She wouldn't have thought she would be interested in someone like him. But she kind of was. Interested. Too bad he'd probably faint if he found out.

～

WEDNESDAY MORNING, Fink squealed the tires as he pulled into the parking lot. The only spaces available were at the far end. He pulled in, not even caring that his car was crooked and took up two spots. He grabbed his briefcase and shot out of the car, feeling bare without a tie. Or a jacket. But he'd barely gotten Wyatt and himself up at all. Calling in sick had been tempting.

Wyatt jogged beside him across the parking lot. "I'll take care of your late notice, just get a pass from Mrs. Herschel and go straight to class," he said as their feet thumped on the blacktop.

Wyatt mumbled something that was drowned out by the familiar roar of a muffler-less pickup. Although today, the pickup slowed down as it pulled in. The tires didn't squeal and all four stayed on the ground. Wyatt and he jogged beside it as it slowed in front of the school, staying off the sidewalk. Harper waved and smiled. Probably she didn't know what to do with her hands since she didn't have to hold on for dear life to keep her head from cracking against the windows.

Fink stopped at the front door and held it open, waiting on Harper and Ellie to get out and walk in. Wyatt walked through the first set of doors and grabbed the second one. This was getting to be a habit.

"Good morning, Harper. Ellie." Man, he loved saying her name.

Her cheeks turned red. It took him a second to notice that not only was she dressed in jeans and a fitted T-shirt, but her hair, well, he wouldn't say it was under control, but she had attempted to tame it into a thick braid that lay down the middle of her back. Frizzy pieces escaped, but they only served to frame her face.

Ellie was slender with curves in the exact right places, adorable pink cheeks, fascinating blue eyes, and those lips— She bit one now as she stood in front of him and he couldn't drag his eyes away. A strange twinge hit his chest, heating up his insides.

He shook his head and moved his gaze over her head. *Stupid man. Pay attention to where you are.* "I'll take care of your note this morning, Ellie. I think I've seen your signature enough times that I can get it right."

Something white waved in front of his face.

"Are you sleepwalking? I just said I had the note. Already written out and signed."

He took the piece of paper. Man, she tied him up in knots. No. He just wasn't getting enough sleep. That was the problem.

"Thanks." One glance told him that Harper and Wyatt had disappeared. "You, ah, look nice today." What had he just said? He clamped down on his tongue. Too late.

She smiled. Her entire face lit up, and he racked his brain for something else to say to keep that smile on her face.

Without a word she reached up. He couldn't move. The world had shrunk to just her, looking at him. Her fingers brushed his neck. Scalding hot. He swallowed. The sides of his throat stuck together. He swallowed again.

Her short breaths puffed on his skin. Minty. Warm. His heart seemed to beat all over his body. His skin felt cool, then clammy.

He almost jumped in surprise when the top button on his shirt popped out of its hole. But he held himself completely still, not wanting to break eye contact, not wanting to lose the ambient magic.

"You'll be more comfortable that way," she whispered.

Her hands started to move back, but he captured her wrists and held them still. For what? He didn't know.

Her bones felt small in his hands. Delicate. Not what he'd expected. He rubbed his thumbs on the insides of her wrists. She worked so hard. And had accepted life, determined to be content and happy. He wanted her to be happy.

"Hey, Mr. F. Are you lift—" Jordon stuck his head out the first set of doors. Thankfully, Fink was partially turned so his back hid most of Ellie. But he opened his hands and released her arms. What was he thinking? They were on school property. Anyone could see.

She took two steps back. Then another. Her smile was gone. She spun on her heel and powerwalked around her truck, before jumping into the cab and cranking on the motor. Soon she was gone in a blast of noise and a cloud of blue smoke.

His heart continued to pound like crazy and his fingers caressed his collar like he could still feel hers on it. Ellie—Mrs. Bright—had touched him. Tenderly. And he'd reacted like a puppy rolling over on the floor with all four paws in the air and its tongue hanging out. He should be ashamed that he had such little self-control.

But he wasn't. Rather, he wanted to run to his car and take off after her, making sure she wasn't angry with him for letting her go. That she hadn't gotten the wrong idea. That she knew he...what? He liked her? He admired her? Respected her?

Crazy chaos. This was Mrs. Bright. Perpetually late. Chronically disorganized. Child-mother.

He scrubbed a hand over his face. Did any of that matter? She had some bad habits—so did he—but the unselfish, caring, funny person under it all had charmed him. She excelled in areas where he lacked. He had a sneaking suspicion their personalities would complement each other perfectly. Maybe he could convince her to give them a try. There had to be an excuse to see her again.

"Mr. F?" Jordon still had his head stuck out the door, while Fink stood staring at the empty road. No smoke from her exhaust remained.

He turned slowly and walked into the school. "Yes, son?"

"Was that Harper's mom?"

"Yes."

"Late again, huh?" Jordon stopped in the hall.

"Not really."

"Oh. Well, okay. I just wanted to know if you were lifting after school today with us."

"The float is done and I should be back on schedule." A life spent with Ellie would probably never run on schedule. Whoa. Where did that thought come from? He wasn't considering spending his life with anyone. Especially Mrs. Bright.

"Okay, I'll look for you tonight, then." Jordon waved and strode off.

Fink stood in the hall. Bemused.

He had to face it. He was attracted to Ellie Bright. Somehow she'd pushed through all the barriers he'd set up in his life, barriers he'd established with the express purpose of keeping himself far from any hint of sexual scandal that could ruin his career. She'd blown right through them. But, currently, he had the superintendent position to consider. He didn't want his conduct to jeopardize that in any way.

He forced his feet to move, greeting Mrs. Herschel before walking into his office. Several papers sat on his desk, and he got busy working through them until a knock sounded on his door.

He startled. Usually Mrs. Herschel announced visitors.

As he stood, he stacked the remaining papers into a pile in the exact center of his desk and glanced at the glass. His brow furrowed. What was the president of the school board doing in his office?

Chapter Eight

"Dr. Rothschild. I wasn't expecting you. Please come in."

Dr. Rothschild gave Fink a professional smile and walked in, her heels clicking on the tile. Her perfume, fancy and cloying, hung in the air. He longed for the fresh scent of pine. He shook his head and looked to make sure someone was behind the desk in the main office. Mrs. Herschel was on the phone, but she smiled and waved.

"Please, sit down." He adjusted one of the chairs, which was out of line with the corner of his desk.

"Thank you." She perched on the edge of her seat. Every piece of her shiny brown hair was perfectly in place. Her face revealed nothing of her thoughts. Even her outfit—a short navy skirt and white blouse—said professional.

"It's a pleasure to see you." Forgive him the white lie. "What can I do for you?"

She blinked and tsked as she opened her mouth. "I'm sorry I didn't call first, but I just got off the phone with several out-of-town guests who are coming to see our little Farmers' Day Parade." Her glossy red lips pulled back, exposing perfect white teeth. He supposed it was a smile.

"I know you are supervising our float, and since these guests...have rather deep pockets"—she lifted a brow, making sure he understood these guests were *rich*, not just rich— "and they are thinking of moving their families to our little school district. Of course they are interested in our academics. However..." She allowed the caveat to hang in the air as her cool blue eyes assessed him.

He resisted the urge to squirm. Pasting a pleasant smile on his face, he adjusted the small stack of papers on his desk, then steepled his fingers over them, waiting for her to continue.

She inhaled through her nose as though smelling something unpleasant. "You do realize that ours is a small district. Few students mean less funding from the state. The two families I spoke with on the phone today have the means to make substantial donations. Donations that could pay for things like new lights and bleachers for the football field. An upgrade to our PA system. A new floor in our gymnasium." She looked down her sharp nose at the cheap veneer on his desk. "New office furniture for the staff."

Silence descended upon the office, broken only by the slow ticking of his large wall clock. Must be his turn to speak. "I am in complete agreement with you. What is it that you want me to do?"

He could entertain these families for the weekend. There were lots of things to do around town. He could take them to Ellie's farm for an evening. Pick out pumpkins, have a hayride, s'mores around a campfire. A genuine smile broke out on his face.

Dr. Rothschild's brows drew together. "I'm so happy to see that you understand the possibilities of this opportunity."

The woman didn't look happy. Fink nodded anyway, and tried to school his features into a more professional demeanor.

"The families will be touring the grounds on Friday. You will eat lunch with them in the staff lounge, but other board members and I will guide their tour." She paused and he could only assume it was for dramatic effect. "You are in charge of the school float for the parade Saturday evening?"

"Yes." He almost added "it's finished," but before he could, she spoke again.

"I do hope you have put some serious effort into it. I'm expecting it to look fabulous. Different, and better, from every other float in the parade." She stared pointedly at Fink.

Fink forced his constricted lungs to take in air. Why, oh why hadn't he listened to Ellie?

"I suspect your float might already be finished. I understand that it would be a horrible inconvenience for you to improve upon your design this close to the parade. I also realize there is a vote next Wednesday on the superintendent position at the regular school board meeting and your name is on the ballot. If the two families visiting us this weekend were to decide to move to our district, I'm certain the results of the vote would please you greatly." Her eyes drilled into him. "But if our school district disappoints in any way..."

"I understand." And, actually, he did. Schools were about students and educating them, but they were also a business. Mixed with politics. It made sense that a principal who could attract money to the school would also be a superintendent who would attract money to the school. A small part of him was aghast at the threat Dr. Rothschild had just barely veiled behind her loaded assumptions. A larger part of him wanted to meet the challenge.

Every part of him wanted to work with Ellie again.

He leaned back in his chair, smiling. Confident. He already had the perfect design for the float. "I will alert the janitorial staff. The school and grounds will be pristine on Friday."

"I will find room in the budget for overtime."

"The students are always well behaved, but I will convey the importance of Friday's visitors to our teachers as well."

"Perfect."

"And the float will be stunning. An inspired work of art."

Dr. Rothschild drew her lips back. "I knew I could count on you, Mr. Finkenbinder."

"Always."

She stood and held out her hand.

He thought about bowing and kissing her knuckles, but he shook it instead, then opened the door and escorted her out. As she walked through the double doors, he glanced at his watch. Lunchtime. He never left the school during the day. Ever. But today, he'd make an exception.

~

ELLIE HUMMED as she pushed the miniature white pumpkin down on the sharpened dowel rod, nestling it among the feathered corn tassels. It contrasted with the brown grapevine wreath structure and deep purple ribbon. Purple had been the most popular color this year. She hadn't always thought of it as a fall color, but obviously someone did.

She twisted the pumpkin, adjusting the angle of the stem. A little touch of green would really make this wreath pop. Where had she set that ivy? Not on the worktable. Not under it. Not on the counter by the cash register. If only Fink were here to keep her organized.

Ah, Fink. He'd looked so handsome this morning. She'd forgotten what rough stubble felt like on her fingers. Had she ever known? She certainly had never felt that tingle in her hand, the swirling of heat in her stomach, the feeling of rightness in her soul.

She picked up a section of ribbon lying on the table. Watching it shimmer in the light, she twirled in the small space between the worktable and the wall, observing it ripple and undulate in the air. Dancing in the small space to keep it waving.

The shop bells tinkled as the door opened. Her foot caught on the doormat. She knocked a can of corn kernels over as she grabbed at the table to keep from falling. They crashed to the floor and splattered.

Capable hands seized her waist, preventing her fall. Helping her stand. Steading her.

Fink.

Her eyes widened. "I was just..." *thinking of you*.

"Yes?" he asked, without releasing her.

"Finishing this wreath." She indicated the purple-ribboned wreath, which had escaped her near-fall unscathed. His familiar spicy scent teased her nose.

"Beautiful," he said.

She shivered and whispered, "You didn't even look at it."

"Look at what?" His gaze dropped to her lips, which she suddenly realized were dry. She touched her tongue to them. His fingers tightened on her waist.

"The wreath."

"What wreath?"

"The one I was just finishing. You said it was beautiful, but you didn't even look at it."

"I wasn't talking about the wreath."

She swallowed. "What were you talking about?"

He opened his mouth.

She moved closer.

Shaking his head as though waking from a dream, he stepped back, dropping his hands from her, shoving them in his pockets. He leaned a shoulder against the open door.

"I have a huge favor to beg of you."

She leaned a hip against the table. Her knees were not overly steady just yet. "I just realized you should be in school. Did you get fired?"

He snorted. "No. Not yet."

"Not yet?"

He took a deep breath, as though needing to focus his thoughts. "You know I've applied for the superintendent position."

"Yes."

"Well, in order for me to secure the position, we need to improve the float. I should have listened to you to begin with, and I'm sorry." He met her eyes. "I was hoping you would help me do the first design. The one I have the picture for?"

"Last time my idea was a complete disaster." She fingered the ribbon in her hand, looking down at it.

"We didn't have directions. I've got to go back to school, but I can see if I can find something on the internet, or maybe the shop teacher, Mr. Woods, might be able to draft me something up."

She looked up. "So you're asking me, not demanding that I do this to keep my daughter out of detention?"

He paused, shoving his hands deeper into his pockets and meeting her eyes. Humbly. "I'm asking. As a friend. For a favor."

"I have an interview with a potential employee scheduled for tonight at seven thirty, but after that I'll do everything I can to help you."

"Thanks. I owe you."

Caught in his eyes, she couldn't look away. Couldn't answer. But she knew her face was shining with a full-on smile. She'd be seeing him again tonight. They'd be working together. She felt like twirling her ribbon again, but resisted the impulse. She'd wait until he left.

"Well, I'd better get back to the school. I'll be out this evening. Eight?"

"Yes."

He made no move to leave.

Each beat of her heart filled her chest with fervor until it threatened to burst.

He pulled his hands out of his pockets and clenched them at his sides.

She twined the ribbon through her fingers.

He took a step closer.

Excitement shimmered in her chest. She leaned toward him.

He closed the distance between them. His hands slid up her cheeks moving into her hair.

His scent surrounded her. Tingles pulsed on her skin. Her knees quivered and her heart rate soared. Time seemed to stop and the world shrank to only them as she touched her tongue to her dry lips.

Fink seemed mesmerized by the movement. Keeping his eyes fixed on her lips, he said, "I thought I might kiss you goodbye?"

She gave a shallow nod, but it was all he needed. He pressed his lips to hers. Just a touch, but sensation rocketed through her body.

He dropped his hands, spun on his heel, and was gone before she opened her eyes.

Chapter Nine

Fink floated on air the rest of the day. He remembered to tell the janitorial staff about the school and grounds for Friday, and sent a group email to all the teachers about the visitors. He went through the motions of his job, but Ellie and the way the sunlight had hit her face and hair this afternoon when he walked in filled his mind. Her beautiful eyes. The delighted expression on her face when she saw him. He could come home to that every day. Easily.

Between thinking about Ellie, he also researched different ways of building the float. By the time he ran into the shed to escape the cold drizzle that evening, he was confident he had plans ready that would work.

Ellie and a young, maybe college-aged, man looked up when he burst in.

"I'm sorry. I didn't realize you were here." He'd figured they'd be up at the office/shop. Or maybe the house. He turned to walk back outside into the drizzle.

"Stay, Fink. We're almost done," Ellie called.

He stepped back in, closing the door behind him.

She turned to the man at her side. "As I was saying, this is the shed where we keep most of our tools." She waved her arm around, indicating the loaded shelves. "Have you ever used a chainsaw?"

"Nope." The kid scratched his head. "Didn't have much need of one in the development where I grew up."

"Okay. You'd have to learn how. The customers are given handsaws to cut their trees down with, but if we have a big order to fill—sometimes we'll load several tractor trailers, especially at the beginning of the season—a handsaw just doesn't cut it."

Fink smiled at her paronomasia, but the kid didn't seem to notice.

"Aren't they kind of dangerous?" The boy shifted on his feet.

Ellie stopped. Fink bit back a snort at her dumbfounded expression.

She ran a hand over her frizzed-out hair. "Well, yeah. You have to be careful."

"I thought working on a Christmas tree farm would be kinda fun. I didn't realize I'd have to cut down trees. Isn't that like destroying Mother Earth?" He bunched his lips together and crossed his arms over his chest.

"We plant new ones. It's fun."

Fink coughed to hide his laugh. Saying "it's fun" through clenched teeth like Ellie just did made her sound like a parent saying spinach really does taste good. "But it's work too. You said you worked at the fast food place in town?"

"Yeah."

"Why are you quitting?"

"Those idiots schedule me to be at work at five thirty in the morning. Normal people don't get out of bed that early. And it's only minimum wage." He slouched against the tractor.

Ellie shook her head. "Have you ever driven a tractor?"

"We had a lawnmower when I was little, but my mom would never let me run it."

"You'd have to learn that too."

Fink dealt with kids like this all the time and was impressed Ellie didn't roll her eyes.

"It's kinda big."

"Yeah. So." Ellie slapped her hands on her pants. "I think that's all. Christmas tree season starts the day after Thanksgiving, although we might have a few big orders to fill before that. I'll give you a call if we're interested."

"Okay." The kid started to turn away, but stopped when Ellie held out her hand. He looked at it for a minute like he wasn't sure what to do with it. Then shook it gingerly.

"Thanks for coming. Can you find your way back up to the parking lot? I've got some work to do here."

"Uh, it was that way?" He pointed in the exact wrong direction.

Fink spoke up. "I'll walk him back up."

Ellie gave him a grateful smile. "Thanks. Would you bring Harper and Wyatt back down with you?"

"Sure. Have you had supper yet?"

"I'll run over to the house and grab a bowl of stew from the Crock-Pot. Have you eaten?"

"Yes." He wanted to reach out and put his arm around her. Her shoulders drooped and there were dark circles under her eyes. A stab of guilt touched his heart. He had asked a lot of her this week. And she had done her best at everything he'd asked. If she'd complained, he hadn't heard it. But he didn't touch her. He might end up kissing her again.

Instead of doing what he really wanted to do, he followed the kid out the door.

Fifteen minutes later, he was back. If Ellie went and got stew, she must have gobbled it down fast, since she was on the wagon, dismantling it when he walked in with Wyatt and Harper. When she saw them, she hopped off with an armload of gourds.

His eyes widened as she placed them back in the groups he had organized, rather than tossing them down wherever. The pumpkins, too, were lined up in neat little rows. She must have done that for him. Because she knew he liked things to be in order. He tucked that idea away to be brought out and examined later.

She stood and smiled at him. He grinned back at her, then placed his briefcase on the back of the wagon and snapped it open. Ellie, Harper, and Wyatt gathered around the back of the wagon.

First, he pulled out the top paper—the completed project. The big moon glowed on the back of the wagon, silhouettes of a man and woman standing face-to-face leaning into each other, but not quite kissing, were solid black against its yellow glow. A dirt road cut through green-and-yellow bucolic fields and seemed to fade off into the bottom of the moon.

"We'll place hay bales here for the king and queen to sit on and throw candy." He pointed to the back of the wagon. "Then we'll have a banner on the back with an advertisement for your farm."

"If we can build that, it's going to look amazing." Wyatt stared at the picture.

"We're going to figure it out, or die trying," Ellie said.

Fink's chest warmed. "Well, I just so happen to have this." He shuffled the papers, pulled out a blueprint to build the base, and laid it on the bed of the wagon so everyone could see. They all bent over it. "I also have this." More shuffling produced three more papers with directions and dimensions on building the moon and covering the base with the scene depicting a dirt road running off in the distance, the massive moon rising directly over where the road disappeared into the horizon.

"This is way too complicated." Wyatt stepped back, shaking his head. Harper nodded.

"It looks that way. But...I've been doing some research, and if we get giant pieces of hardboard, there won't need to be much support to get the moon that high because it won't weigh much, even though it's huge. Same with the 'walls' of the base. The only things I was unsure of were how to get a light to shine on the moon, and how to get that picture on the hardboard. I think it's too late to order screen printing."

"Mom can do it. Easy," Harper spoke up.

"She can paint that scene?" Fink tried not to show his astonishment.

"She can paint anything. She's an amazing artist."

Ellie tilted her head to the side, her lips pulled back. "If that's as big as it looks, it's going to take a massive amount of paint. And time."

Fink shook his head. "I was afraid of that. Maybe we could look into the screen printing."

"That's going to be expensive," Ellie stated.

"I know. But there is a budget for this and I might be able to get more." Dr. Rothschild was pretty eager to impress her visitors. "But since we don't have to buy any lumber...."

"I think if I had maybe twelve, eighteen hours, I could do it." Ellie twisted a stray strand of hair. "But this is Wednesday night. I don't know where I could find the time."

"Where are we going to get the hardboard?" Wyatt spoke up from Fink's other side. "Won't that be expensive?"

"Good question," Ellie said. "I have some particle board around here. Maybe a few sheets of plywood, but not enough and no hardboard."

"Mrs. Herschel's brother works at the hardboard factory outside of town. Turns out this weekend they had a machine malfunction and cut the sheets an inch or so too short." Fink adjusted the papers on his briefcase. It had been a stroke of tremendous luck that Mrs. Herschel had overheard his conversation and suggested hardboard. "They've got a dumpster out back and it's full of perfect sheets that are just a little too short for specs. Which wouldn't matter to us at all. The top pieces might be a bit wet from the rain yesterday, but we can dig down. He said there was a ton, and anyone was welcome to go and take what they wanted."

Ellie narrowed her eyes at him. "You just suggested we pick stuff out of a dumpster?"

"Hardboard." Honestly, he was surprised that this woman who walked around perpetually disorganized, dodging masses of junk, would take umbrage at the idea of pulling something out of a dumpster. "The store manager wouldn't keep it out for us."

"I can't believe you suggested *dumpster diving*." She moved her hands in a now-I've-seen-everything gesture.

"It's just hardboard." Fink's nervousness morphed into irritation. He had beaten down his compunctions on rooting through what amounted to trash so that they could do this project. He was the neat freak. Not her.

"But there could be needles or vomit or, or, *anything* in there."

Fink's chest ballooned with that familiar, strong emotion. He almost welcomed it. He noticed the color and lights in Ellie's eyes, and wondered if she felt it too.

He stepped toward her. Raising his voice, he said, "I spent all this time researching and all you can do is complain?"

"I'm not complaining. I'm just shocked." Her voice had raised to not quite a shout.

"Well, I didn't see you coming up with anything." He finished closing the distance between them and stood directly in front of her. That feeling, not exactly anger, but big and large and gripping, burst inside him.

"That's because I don't have massive amounts of time to sit around and twiddle my perfectly manicured thumbs." She stepped up on a pumpkin by her feet. Her face was now even with his. Her finger jammed in front of his nose. Possibly she was in the grip of the same emotion he was.

"Lady, your hands don't know the meaning of the word *manicure*," he shouted.

"I didn't mean it as a compliment," she shouted right back, looking him straight in the eye. Her chest heaved in and out. She touched her tongue to the corner of her lip.

Anticipation lit his insides. This was where they grabbed each other and...

"Mom. Mr. F. Please." Harper pushed herself between them, a hand up in front of both their faces.

What was it about this woman? She got him hot faster than anyone he'd ever met. He'd actually been enjoying that argument.

"Seriously guys. I think that dumpster diving for hardboard sounds like a load of fun. And I think Wyatt would help me. But I'm afraid to leave you two alone. I thought you were kissing Monday night when we walked in, but now I think it's possible you two were putting some weird, twisted WWE moves on each other."

"I kinda thought the whole scaffolding falling down was suspect," Wyatt offered hesitantly. "It makes more sense to me that they were fighting and crashed into it."

"It's a shame I can't leave my own mother alone with the high school principal. What kind of adult am I going to turn out to be?" Harper crossed her arms over her chest and mock glared at her mother. Not disrespectfully, but half-playful, half-annoyed.

Ellie stepped down from the pumpkin, reminding Fink of a queen descending from her royal conveyance. But her apology was sincere. "I'm sorry. I lost my temper."

"Boy howdy," Harper said. "And I don't even think you two were insulting each other at first. Not on purpose. Mom was just saying she couldn't believe you were going to these extremes to make what she wanted. And you were just saying you'd put a lot of time into it."

They eyed each other. Why did he have such a hard time controlling himself around this woman? His lips lifted at the thought. She grinned back at him.

The kids must not have noticed their cheesy smiles, because Wyatt said, "I have an idea about the painting. Uncle Fink can leave school and come here and work on the farm, waiting on customers and whatever, for Mrs. Bright. That way she can come down here and paint."

Fink's heartbeat settled into a regular rhythm. The feeling that had swelled in his throat was gone. Was it passion? It had been so long since he'd allowed himself to feel anything, he wasn't quite sure. But he was sure he couldn't allow himself to feel it for Ellie. Not now.

Focus on the conversation. "That's a great idea, Wyatt. I could actually leave the school early for the next two days. Maybe by two thirty." He turned to Ellie. "Would that help?"

She stared at the papers, then looked up, mumbling to herself. Finally, she stopped and faced him. "I think that would give me enough time. I can buy the paint tomorrow when I go to town. I'd want to see the hardboard first, but I think I can use a spray paint base."

"Wyatt and I can go get the hardboard now. Can you two keep from killing each other until we get back?"

Mrs. Bright shuffled her feet and peeked up at him. "You were right about the manicure. I've never actually had one. I don't know why your comment made me so angry."

"Well, you were right too. I do have some free time in the afternoon. And lunch. And my free period at school." He put a hand on Wyatt's shoulder. "We'll be fine. We'll start the base, and if you two bring the hardboard back, we might be able to tack it up in place tonight before we knock off."

Chapter Ten

After Harper and Wyatt left, Ellie and Fink fell into the rhythm of the night before, only this time in addition to keeping the tools organized and sawing after she measured, Fink also read the instructions, making sure they had the right number of boards cut to the proper length.

They had worked in silence for ten minutes when Fink spoke. "You've done a good job with Harper."

The tape measure snapped shut, pinching her thumb. Pain poked up her arm. The tape measure bobbled in her hand before she tightened her grip on it. "Thanks. She was a good kid, and it didn't take much. How'd you end up with Wyatt? He seems sweet."

"He is. My sister traveled the globe, writing for different magazines. She also worked odd jobs to support her love of travel and adventure. Wyatt's been everywhere—I wasn't always sure how he'd turn out—but she did a great job chasing her dreams and parenting too. He's respectful, and there's an innocence to him...."

"Almost like he was homeschooled."

"Yeah. I think he was, to some extent," Fink said. "Harper has hinted several times about you being young when you had her. How old were you?"

She didn't want to answer. She wanted to keep pretending there might be a chance for something between them to blossom.

"Hand me the saw, please."

He picked it up, but when she reached for it, he didn't let go.

She tugged.

He held on. "How old?"

"Fifteen." She yanked the saw out of his hand, waiting for the gasp and horrified gaze.

His expression did not change. Unsmiling, he stared into her face, like she was a puzzle he needed to solve. "Did you think of giving her up?"

"Sure. My parents wanted me to. Actually, they wanted me to have an abortion. But, hey, I was fifteen. And stupid. I was almost six months along before I realized I wasn't just gaining weight from pizza and soda."

"So no abortion?"

"It would have been hard, if not impossible. But I wouldn't have done it anyway. Liam and I got married instead and we moved in with his parents." She pounded a nail in.

He handed her another. "You regret that?"

"Surprisingly, no. My parents were both professionals—Mom worked in public relations and was gone a lot. Dad retired from the army and drank a lot. I was the baby of their old age; they were almost fifty when I was born." It had been a lonely childhood. Maybe that's why she had clung to Liam. Trying to fill the emptiness left by the absence of her parents.

"No brothers or sisters?"

"Nope. Wished for them, but never happened." She finished pounding the nail and set the hammer down.

He moved it after placing the tape measure in her hand. "Harper mentioned wanting siblings."

"That'd be a little hard, since my husband's dead."

He didn't say anything.

She marked the board and snapped the tape measure shut, feeling bad about being abrupt. "Liam and I planned on it. I wanted to get my GED first. But you know how you get busy. Life happens. Harper needed me. Then I started working on the farm. Then he was killed."

"A paving accident?" He handed her the SKILSAW.

She cut the board, the shrill of the saw filling the barn. The end piece fell off, clattered on the floor, and the saw wound down to silence before she asked, "You checked up on me?"

"It's a small school. Small community. I hear rumors." He handed her the hammer and a nail, then picked up the piece she'd cut off and stacked it with the rest of the scraps.

"He ran the big roller on the paving crew. He must not have been paying attention and he ran it far enough off the road that it tipped. They were on a big hill, and once it tipped, it belly-rolled clear down the hill. First roll killed him instantly." She paused to reflect. It'd been devastating. She'd built so much of her life around him. But it had happened ten years ago, and the hurt had mostly healed, leaving an empty space that would probably always be there.

"Wow. So you had a young child and no husband."

She stopped and looked him in the eyes, conscious of his occupation. An education had to be high on his list of priorities in a partner. "No job and not even a high school diploma. But he left me his parents. They've been the parents I never had and they've been great with Harper."

"So you helped on the farm."

"Never thought I'd be a farmer, but that's how it turned out." She laughed without humor, taking the nail he handed her.

"You seem to like it."

"I do. Now that we sell decorations, I get to use my artistic abilities, but I love being outside, love growing things, and I love that Harper has a good, stable home, even if we do work a lot."

"So that's why you had that kid there? Hoping to take some of the load off?"

"I guess."

He snorted. "I've really added to that load this week."

"It'll be good advertising for the farm. We're just not quite making enough money to hire full-time help. The Christmas season is the busiest time of year for us, retail-wise, anyway, and if there's someone here helping with all that, I'll have more time to make crafts."

"That's a pretty big business for you."

"Sure, it's all up-market." She shrugged. "And I love it, of course."

"Art is your passion."

"Yeah. What I'd really like is to have help all summer, trimming the Christmas trees and spraying the apples, taking care of the vegetables so I can get ahead with the decorations. That was my main thought with interviewing Cody. He's still in college and I figured he'd be looking for full-time work next summer."

She reached for the tape measure he held, but instead of handing it to her, he captured her hand in his own.

Her gaze shot to his. He couldn't be serious about her. Couldn't be. Fink didn't seem like the kind of guy to mess with her, but neither did he seem like the kind of guy who would settle for a woman who was uneducated, messy, and perpetually late.

"Please don't, Fink."

He dropped her hand. "I'm sorry," he murmured. "Seems like every time I get around you, I want to get closer."

"I have the same want," she whispered. "But you and I...it's not something that could ever happen." She searched his eyes, whether looking for confirmation or denial, she wasn't sure. *Please, Fink, tell me I'm wrong.* When he didn't say anything, her gaze fell and she looked away. There was her answer.

This afternoon when he'd asked to kiss her goodbye, she'd thought that maybe her background wouldn't matter to him.

Swallowing something that tasted an awful lot like disappointment, she said, "Are you going to give me the tape measure, or have you abducted it?"

He cleared his throat, putting it into her outstretched hand. "Sorry."

They worked in silence for a while, and Ellie managed to get her runaway emotions under control. Served her right for practically demanding to know what his intentions were.

Of course he couldn't come right out and say it, but he really didn't have to. She might not have a degree, any degree, but she wasn't stupid.

Her chest felt wooden and her movements jerky. She could tell herself Fink's rejection didn't matter all day long, but she wasn't fooling herself. It stung. It was her own dumb fault for allowing herself to care for someone whom she knew from the get-go could never return her feelings. She bit the insides of her cheeks and tried to ignore the ache in her chest. It wasn't the first disappointment in her life. Wouldn't be the last.

She couldn't take the silence any longer. "You came from Iowa. How'd you end up here in PA?"

~

FINK PICKED up the hammer Ellie had set down and placed it to the side. "I grew up on a farm in Iowa. But I chose to leave it. I couldn't get away fast enough." He straightened the hammer a fraction of an inch. Satisfied with the exact position of the handle, parallel to the other tools, he rubbed the back of his neck and sighed. "Then, my mom got sick. My dad asked me to go back and help them so they wouldn't lose the farm." He swallowed and shook his head. "I chose my career."

"Oh, wow."

He knew his face had closed down, an involuntary reaction when he didn't want to show his true feelings, although he spoke casually, without looking at her. Not wanting her to know how deep those feelings ran.

"Yeah. She died. And losing the farm killed Dad, not right away, but within a year. And every day I regret that."

Her hands hung suspended in midair. Like she'd been reaching for something, but had forgotten what. Her face shone with compassion. "That regret hasn't stopped you from moving up in your career?"

"I made my choice. Now I get to live with it." His lips flattened. "I graduated from Penn State and got a job here teaching science. I got my master's degree and was hired for the principal position when it opened. I'm working on my doctorate."

"Wow." She didn't sound happy. "You're close?"

"Yes. My dissertation should be complete by Christmas. Unless I have to make more floats."

She snorted. "Once you have your degree, you've got a job in mind?"

He met her gaze and raised a brow. He'd told her earlier today.

Her brow furrowed before the light dawned. She rolled her eyes. "So that's why you're here. You're up for superintendent and you need to make sure the school has a float in the parade. Because, after all, we country folk are kind of anal about our parades."

"True."

He noted the hopeless tone in her voice. Maybe the fact she didn't even have a high school diploma and he was close to getting his doctorate mattered to her. He couldn't tell. Heck, a week ago, it would have mattered to him. Now, not so much.

Once he had the superintendent job, his wife not having her high school diploma wouldn't matter to him and should be no one else's business.

But the thing that kept him silent...him being with her now, before the vote...that could sway someone's opinion. Someone might think less of him for being with her.

He thought of Dr. Rothschild, her tight lips, and how she regarded anything that wasn't completely perfect with intense disapproval. He knew right away that it *would* matter to her.

Could it cost him the job? She was just one vote, but she was also the school board president, and highly respected in the community. She might campaign against him. He didn't think she would, but he didn't want to take that chance. He didn't know the other members well enough to say for sure if they would care.

Ellie was well liked by folks in the county, he knew that much. But that was taking an awful big chance—basing his career on how much people liked her. His brain said to let her go.

After the vote, though, different story. Was it wrong to wait until next Thursday? To think he had time might be too egotistical. Ellie had become too important to lightly dismiss. He'd talk to her next Thursday, and do whatever it took to get her to agree to take a chance on him. Because although it terrified him, he'd realized what this crazy feeling he had for Ellie was. Love.

～

THURSDAY MORNING FINK pulled into the school parking lot. A little slower than he had the past two days, because he wasn't late. Yet. The bell was going to ring in three minutes, but he couldn't speed in the parking lot. Kids were still hurrying inside the building. It would be a bad example.

As he pulled his briefcase out of the backseat, the low rumble of Ellie's pickup cut through the clear morning air. Funny how that noise used to be annoying. It now made him smile. She, too, drove only a fraction of her normal speed. Harper waved at kids who yelled at her through the window. The second day in a row she hadn't had to hang on for dear life.

Fink quickened his pace so he could open Ellie's door for her. If Harper hopped out quickly, she wouldn't be late. Harper was no fool, and as Fink leaned against Ellie's window and the bell rang, she was already following Wyatt into the school.

Ellie wound her window down with the crank. "I guess I won't need this." She held up a white piece of paper with writing he assumed was Harper's late excuse and tore it into pieces, her eyes aglow with life and laughter.

Fink found himself leaning in the window toward her, drawn to the happiness and vivacity she exuded. He stopped himself from reaching for her but didn't step away.

"You look nice." She wore a scooped-neck, pink blouse and a blue skirt.

Her cheeks pinked. "I have to run to town and grab some paint. My in-laws can probably handle the farm unless we get a last-minute group in, and I should be able to paint all day."

"Great." He stared into her eyes, almost forgetting what he was going to say. "I'll be out to help as soon as I can."

"They'll be expecting you." She glanced down. Her lips pulled back and one brow lifted. "You look good too."

She stared at his biceps. His agreement with Jordon had actually helped him bulk up some, and it was possible he'd set his arm on her window hoping she'd notice.

"I thought I'd go casual today since I'll be going straight to the farm after school." He'd worn a polo shirt and slacks. There was no dress code, so he might as well.

"I like it," she said softly.

He stood there, grinning like a fool for too long, before remembering he needed to get into the school. "Have a good day." He stepped back.

"You too," she said, then shifted into gear and chugged out of the parking lot.

~

FINK LEFT the school immediately after the kids were dismissed. He caught himself going forty-three in a thirty-five-mile-per-hour zone. He couldn't remember the last time he'd speeded.

His stomach churned with excitement as Wyatt and he pulled into the tree farm. He didn't even try to pretend he wasn't looking for Ellie. His head swiveled in every direction. Probably fifty people milled about in the pumpkin patch and corn maze, with a few scattered around eating hot dogs and dodging the campfire smoke. Children jumped in the leaves that had fallen from the red maples by the shop.

He didn't see Ellie.

Fink and Wyatt stepped into the office. Ellie's mother-in-law greeted them.

"I'm Calvin Finkenbinder. I told Ellie I'd help out today and tomorrow so she could paint."

She bustled over, dusting her hands off on her apron. "I'm Esther. I've been expecting you. Let me finish up here, then I'll show you a few things and get you started. With the warm weather we've been having, the corn maze has been popular, and we've had brisk business all week. Except yesterday evening. Things clear out quickly when it rains." She laughed, a tinkling sound that made Fink smile.

He concealed his disappointment that Ellie wasn't there to show him what to do.

Esther rearranged a few wreathes on the display table. "I wish Ellie had time to replenish her supply of fall decorations. We're almost out." She placed her hands on her hips, tilting her head and studying her handiwork. "A local church is bringing a group of folks out tonight, so we're going to be especially busy." Her gaze landed on Wyatt standing at the edge of the doorway and she stopped short. "Are you here to help too?"

He nodded.

"That's great. Harper just walked down to fill the tubs with water for apple bobbing. You scoot on down and she'll put you to work."

A corner of Wyatt's mouth lifted. He turned, tripping on his extra-large feet, but caught himself before he sprawled down the wooden steps.

"Mr. Finkenbinder, how about you step over here and I'll show you the price list."

He fought down impatience and irritation as he strode over to Esther. He'd come to help so Ellie could work on the float, but a small part of him wanted her to miss him as much as he missed her. For her to be here, looking for him, eager to see him too.

Chapter Eleven

Fink's feet hurt, his back ached, and he was starving by the time things slowed down around seven. But he'd had fun. Several old, large red maple trees, their leaves a brilliant orange, shaded the shop, and he'd spent thirty minutes jumping in a big pile of fallen leaves with a group of toddlers.

He hadn't had that much fun in ages. Crisp fall air, brilliant blue sky, perfect bright orange trees still frosted with green. A whiff of woodsmoke and hot dogs. Brisk exercise and the laughter of children. Life was good. He was tired, sore, and dirty, but happy. Joyful, in a way he hadn't been in a long, long time. Since before he'd left the farm.

He'd been surprised to see dozens of kids from the high school there too. The place could almost be considered a hangout. Kids seemed to love the corn maze, and many of them spent several hours hanging around the fire. He'd even seen some of them jumping in the leaves after he'd gone to help a family carry pumpkins from the patch. His heart had swelled to see how they'd accepted Wyatt. Of course, that might have had something to do with Harper. Smart and popular, she'd helped Wyatt fit in fast at his new school. And as Fink worked throughout the afternoon and evening, she kept Wyatt busy with jobs that allowed him to be near her and also interact with the other teenagers loitering around the farm.

A family with several small children pulled in and walked to the pumpkin patch. The mother carried an infant. The father had a toddler on his hip. Their other two small children ran around through the pumpkin patch, laughing and falling. Fink let them alone for a while, but kept an eye on them, and when the father tried to juggle the toddler in one hand and pick up a pumpkin in the other, Fink walked out and offered to help.

Ten minutes later, they had at last made their final decisions, and he balanced four pumpkins in his arms, using his chin as a levering agent to keep them from tumbling out. He started picking his way back.

Two ladies walked down the path, and he stepped aside to allow them to pass. An itch on his cheek distracted him.

"Mr. Finkenbinder?" He froze, his cheek pressed to a pumpkin. And still itchy. But he quickly forgot about that because he was pretty sure the voice was Dr. Rothschild's.

As he turned his head to look, he straightened, trying to appear as scholarly as possible.

"Dr. Rothschild. How nice to see you." Flat-out lie.

She wrinkled her nose. "Mrs. Rosencrantz, this is Mr. Finkenbinder, our high school principal."

The lady Dr. Rothschild had introduced looked much more relaxed than her host. She smiled, a genuine friendly smile, and waved back at a man and four children straggling along behind her.

"Hey, honey. This is the school principal." She said *school principal* like a teenaged girl might have said some hot movie actor's name. She even giggled and kind of bounced with her knees. They couldn't be the VIPs Dr. Rothschild had said were coming for the weekend.

"I was just helping out here so Mrs. Bright could help paint the float." Fink wasn't sure why he felt compelled to explain to Dr. Rothschild. Most assuredly it had to do with the superintendent position and possibly guilt over Ellie. Although he had no reason to feel guilt over Ellie. He closed his mouth.

The man caught up to his wife, and their kids crowded around. Two of the children looked old enough to be in the high school, which housed the seventh through twelfth grades since there was no middle school.

"I see," Dr. Rothschild muttered.

"Hey, Mr. F. Need some help with those?" Harper jogged up, with Wyatt following behind. They grabbed the pumpkins from Fink while he pointed to the family to whom they belonged.

"No problem. We'll take care of them." Harper started walking away, but Wyatt stopped in front of the oldest boy.

"Hey, don't I know you from somewhere?" he asked.

The boy squinted, then his eyes widened in recognition. "You're Wyatt! We skied together in the Andes. You were on my soccer team."

"Yeah. And you're Richard." Wyatt couldn't throw an arm around him, since he held two pumpkins, but he said, "Come on up to the shop with me. We'll catch up."

The boy strode off, his mouth moving the whole time.

His parents gave each other a concerned look.

"I think they'll be fine. That was my nephew," Fink said.

"He seems to be recovering well from his mother's death," Mrs. Rosencrantz said.

"You knew my sister?"

"She occasionally worked at our ski resort. In the town of Farellones in the Andes Mountains of Chile."

Fink stood and talked to the Rosencrantzes for a good half hour, finding out that they loved his sister and she had been well liked in Chile and that Wyatt had been especially beloved. They also mentioned they sold their ski resort so their children could graduate from schools in America, but they wanted to all be together, and they also wanted to settle in a rural area.

"This town seems ideal," Mrs. Rosencrantz said.

"And finding Wyatt here...we didn't know the name of the town you lived in, but your sister talked about visiting you and how beautiful Pennsylvania is this time of year. She was absolutely right."

Dr. Rothschild made a show of glancing at her watch. "It's almost closing time. We'll be seeing Mr. Finkenbinder tomorrow." She ushered them toward the pumpkin patch with promises of catching up more at lunch the next day.

Fink went to the pole building to empty the apple-bobbing tubs and tidy up, relieved the Rosencrantzes seemed to be nice people and had really seemed enthused about their small community. The school board should be happy to hear that.

By the time he stepped into the shop/office, the campfire was out and the last customer was pulling out of the parking lot. Esther shooed him out, saying she would take care of the cash register and cleaning up and asking him to take soup from the Crock-Pot in the kitchen down to the shed for Ellie.

"When she gets her head in an art project, she doesn't remember to come up for air, let alone food," Esther said.

Fink thought about that as he walked from the shop to the house. Ellie definitely had an artist's personality. They were opposites. They'd drive each other crazy.

Opposites attract.

Which, of course, explained why he had such a hard time ignoring his feelings. The crazy pull that she had on him. Why he couldn't stop thinking about her kiss. Couldn't stop wanting to kiss her again. He really needed to get a handle on this runaway attraction. Brushing a last clinging leaf off his pants pocket with his elbow, he pushed open the shed door, careful not to spill the bowls of beef stew.

Ellie stood on the wagon with her back to him, her hourglass figure accented by her fitted T-shirt and jeans, her hair in a braid hanging down her back. Flyaway tendrils frizzed around her head.

His heart thumped as his eyes savored. He'd missed her today. He was tempted to forget his career and tell her right now that he longed to be near her and hoped she felt the same. But he pushed that idea aside. A week. He only had to wait a week until he could declare his feelings and hope she returned them.

His gaze moved to the area where she worked. From the way Harper had talked, he'd expected a masterpiece to be on the hardboard. But it wasn't. He didn't think it was, anyway. Not like he was an art expert. He'd been a science major.

The hardboard was no longer brown. It was white. And not flat any longer, but ridged and bumpy. Textured.

She finally saw him, and stopped. Her eyes widened when she saw the food, and he thought he heard her stomach growl.

"I didn't realize until just now that I'm starving." She set the tools down and rinsed her hands off in a bucket of water. Her work area had things strewn everywhere. Paper, tools, water, bowls, brushes, and towels were all scattered haphazardly. Everything was splattered with a white, plaster-like substance. He smiled to himself. She needed him.

"Come on down. This stew smells delicious."

She finished drying her hands on a plaster-splattered towel and hopped off the wagon. "Aren't you going to ask why I'm not painting?"

"Aren't you going to tell me?"

"Now that you asked…I decided last night, after I went to bed, that it would look more realistic if I added texture. But I needed a medium that would dry fast, although it doesn't necessarily have to be super strong or durable. After all, we're going to use it in the float, then it's bye-bye to everything, right?" She stopped in front of him and tilted her head.

"Yes. I don't see any point in keeping it. We make a new float every year." He refrained from wiping the spot of white plaster off the tip of her nose and handed her the bowl of stew instead.

"Thanks," she said, taking the bowl. Their fingers brushed and little patters of electric shock tumbled up his hand. "That's what I thought. So, anyway, the stuff I'm using fits the bill. I've got it textured like grass, and by the time we're done eating, we should be able to start painting."

He pulled his gaze from her lips and looked again at the white hardboard. "I see the textures you're talking about. Looks like ridges running vertical."

She nodded and swallowed. "Not straight, though. If you notice, the ridges are bent, like grass waving in the wind."

"I see it."

"I've got to get this done tonight, though, because tomorrow night we open the haunted barn."

"I forgot. I was kind of hoping to see you at the football game." One tendril of hair curled by her cheek, and he clenched his fingers into a fist to keep from twirling it around his finger.

"Oh no. I definitely can't make that." She sighed, looking at her bowl. "We'll be shorthanded this weekend for the haunted barn because of Homecoming. Two of the five kids who help out have already taken Friday and Saturday off." Her shoulders slumped and she bit her lip.

He had to go to the football game. He had to be at the dance too. "What about the parade Saturday evening? I assumed you'd be there."

"No. The haunted barn starts at dark."

Why was he so disappointed Ellie wouldn't be at the parade? Maybe because they'd spent so much time working on the float together, he just assumed they'd watch it together.

She set her empty bowl aside. "You know, I was thinking about that moon, that a frame with see-through white material stretched over it would be neat, and if we had some kind of stand, there could be a real couple silhouetted behind it, rather than cutouts."

"I like that idea." The experience he'd gotten this week had maybe bolstered his confidence. "I don't think that would be hard to make."

She grinned. "Me either."

"How about I see if I can search for some ideas on the internet. My laptop's in my briefcase in my car."

"Sounds good." Her eyes crinkled as he picked up her bowl. "Missed you today."

His heart leaped in his chest. Then it settled when he realized she was talking about him cleaning up for her. "Every time I come back, you're surrounded by another disaster area."

"That's my life."

FRIDAY MORNING, Ellie parked in front of Fink's office just as the bell rang. Harper had already jumped out, and when the bell stopped, the door was closing behind her.

Through his office window, she saw Fink standing beside his desk surrounded by at least ten people. He'd mentioned something about families visiting today, so Ellie assumed they were the folks he was talking about. A stab of disappointment cut through her, and she smiled sadly at how pathetic she was. She'd actually put on nice clothes —a pair of beige slacks and a blue ruffled blouse that made her eyes look extra blue—and took the time to somewhat tame her hair. For what? It wasn't like she had a chance with him or anything.

She should drive away. There was no reason to stay or get out, but her hands rested on the steering wheel. She smiled as a child in his office took a Tootsie Roll from the candy container, and Fink reached down to straighten it without taking his eyes from the man speaking to him.

She looked at her hands.

They'd finished the float last night. Everything was ready for whoever was crowned king and queen, and Harper and Wyatt had agreed to ride on the float on the platform behind the moon and be the silhouettes. Fink hadn't said anything about coming over tonight after the game, and she'd be busy anyway. She wouldn't see him until tomorrow at the parade.

Well, she wasn't getting anything done here. She put her pickup in gear and eased out, unable to resist one last look in Fink's window. He had turned his head, and their eyes met as she pulled away from the curb. Heat curled in her belly, and her chest tightened.

His lips turned up and he nodded once. She lifted a hand. Then she was past his window. Feeling like she was leaving a part of herself behind, she deliberately pushed on the accelerator.

Chapter Twelve

Ellie sat in her little shop finishing up her fourth wreath of the day, when her phone buzzed with a text. She jumped, knocking a spool of ribbon onto the floor.

"Drat," she muttered as she scrambled after it, not wanting it to get dirty as it rolled out over the floor. Her phone continued to buzz while she caught the ribbon and rolled it back up.

Both texts were from Harper.

I am Homecoming queen!

The second one was in all caps.

THE KING IS WYATT!

Ellie squealed and did a little happy dance. Harper had never said anything about wanting to be queen, and Ellie suspected she didn't really care. But Wyatt had struggled to fit in at the beginning of the year, and the fact he'd been voted king said to her that he'd managed to make the adjustment quite well.

> Congratulations!

She texted back, then realized Harper and Wyatt were supposed to stand behind the moon, but they'd be sitting as king and queen on the float.

Mom and Dad would probably be willing to be the silhouettes on the float. All she had to do was find someone else to help with the haunted house.

Her stomach growled. Lunchtime. But she wanted to finish this last wreath before she knocked off. Usually there were enough customers after lunch to prohibit any meaningful work getting done.

She had just tightened the elaborate orange bow when her phone buzzed again.

A text from Fink.

> Harper probably told you Wyatt and she are Homecoming king and queen. You and I can stand behind the moon.

Ellie smiled. She read the text again, just because it was from Fink. Then, deciding she'd make something work out with the personnel at the farm, she answered.

> That's fine.

Almost immediately Fink texted back.

> I have a surprise for the float. I'll bring it over after the game. You can put me to work.

What surprise could he have?

> You bet I will. You can rescue lost kids from the corn maze. There are always a lot of them on weekend nights.

She hesitated before adding:

> What surprise???

> You'll see.

She chuckled, sure that it wouldn't matter how much she begged. If Fink didn't want to tell her, he wouldn't be persuaded. Soon another text came through.

> Come to the game at halftime to see Harper crowned. I'll meet you at the gate.

This was a once-in-a-lifetime event for Harper. The farm would just have to make do without her for an hour while she went to see her daughter. She typed back:

> OK. Give me the surprise then?

> Nope.

She shook her head at her phone. Crazy man. Anticipation lit her insides and not wholly because of Harper being queen. She couldn't wait to see Fink.

Chapter Thirteen

Ellie squinted from the glare of the bright lights and scanned the crowd at the gate, searching for Fink's distinctive dark hair. The smell of hotdogs mixed with the tangy scent of fall leaves. Kids of various ages ran around. Younger ones played on the monkey bars, laughing, yelling, and chasing each other, here to play with their friends and not to watch the football game.

Just like she'd done ever since Ellie had been in school, Mrs. Herschel took tickets at a brightly lit table under a canopy tent. A hundred yards away, down the hill and across the field, the crowd cheered. The loudspeaker crackled with a man's excited voice. The field lights cut through the darkness, giving the impression of daylight. She checked out the people coming and going between the field and the gate. There weren't many, and Fink was not among them.

"Hello, Mrs. Herschel," Ellie said as she stepped up to the table.

"Ellie, dear. Mr. Finkenbinder said you might be coming." Mrs. Herschel slid her glasses down her nose and searched the area around the field as Ellie had just done. "I don't see him right now, and I do know he had a group of people to entertain." Her kind hazel eyes landed back on Ellie. "How are you, dear?" The wind ruffled her curly silver hair. She hunched down deeper into her baby-blue sweatshirt.

Ellie smiled. "I'm fine."

"When Mr. Finkenbinder mentioned you, I was a little surprised. I never thought you two got along that well." She looked over her glasses at Ellie.

"We've been working together on the float this week, and we've declared a truce of sorts." What she felt for Fink went deeper than a truce, but getting into it with Mrs. Herschel would be uncomfortable. Just standing here in the noise and the dark and the wind and the smells took her back eighteen years. She had a vague sense of being a lost kid, pregnant, alone, and scared.

She shrugged the feeling off. She was an adult now, and had successfully raised that unexpected blessing. Today she had nothing to be uncomfortable about. "I'll just mosey down. Tell him I was here if he shows up."

"If you wait, honey, I'll go with you. We don't charge people after the second quarter."

Ellie glanced at the tent and the table. "Are you taking the stuff down?"

"Yes. And I have to run the cash box over and lock it in my trunk."

"You do that, and I'll have this down by the time you get back."

After taking the table and the tent down, she set them by the fence. Then she unplugged the light and wound up the extension cord.

Look at that neat pile. Wouldn't Fink be proud of her?

Squinting down the hill, she still didn't see him.

"Oh, that's perfect, dear. Thanks so much. That canopy is a bear for me to get down by myself." Mrs. Herschel shuffled back.

"It was kind of heavy. I can't believe you do it by yourself."

"Actually, honey, I don't. Usually Mr. Finkenbinder and Jordon are here to help. Sometimes he has a whole crowd of boys around him. I seldom lift a finger." She chuckled as they started down the hill.

Fink hadn't really struck her as the type of school administrator who was popular with the students. But, come to think of it, Harper had always liked him. And, come to think of it again, kids often tapped his office window and waved at him. She'd assumed they did it to irritate him, leaving handprints and all. But maybe they did it because they liked him.

"You know, Mr. Finkenbinder is a good man. But he's always alone. I worry about him."

Mrs. Herschel stumbled a bit, and Ellie said, "Here, grab my arm."

"Oh, you're sweet." Her gloved fingers gripped tighter than Ellie would have thought possible. "But with his nephew showing up this fall..."

Curious about the secretary's perspective on him, Ellie listened closely.

"Now today, he has me looking for his lady friend. That's never happened before either. I think you and Mr. Finkenbinder could work out. You'll soften his rough edges and he'll give you structure." Mrs. Herschel sighed the sigh of old-lady matchmakers everywhere.

Ellie didn't have the heart to remind Mrs. Herschel that she wasn't good enough for Fink. She didn't want to say it at all. It hurt to think that she didn't measure up. That she needed a piece of paper attached to her name to make her worthy.

She steadied Mrs. Herschel as they crossed a small ditch and headed toward the home-side bleachers. The crowd cheered and her head turned toward the field.

Of course, she could leave the farm and take art classes. Now that Harper was graduating in the spring, she was no longer tied to the farm for her daughter. Harper was already accepted at Penn State, and she planned to commute for the first year, so she'd be around to help with the farm.

If she went after her art dream, she would have to leave her in-laws with all the farmwork. She wasn't sure she wanted to do that. The thought caused a vague uneasiness to slide through her. Art school might have been her dream at one time, but it wasn't what she wanted anymore. She loved the farm and, if she were honest, didn't want to leave.

They stopped at the foot of the crowded bleachers.

"Oh, there he is." Mrs. Herschel pointed to a group of well-dressed people at the bottom of the stands. Fink sat beside a woman in an elegant dressy coat.

Ellie's heart seized. *Dr. Danielle Rothschild.* Until Ellie had dropped out, they'd been in the same class. Friends in elementary school.

Competitors in high school. Enemies after Liam choose Ellie over Danielle.

Even from here, Ellie could see that her hair was perfectly coffered. It shone in the lights. She held herself with an aristocratic bearing that bespoke confidence and class. Danielle said something and Fink laughed. Ellie's chest tightened. Maybe she didn't particularly want to go to art school, or even to leave the farm, but she wasn't sure she wanted to stay and be reminded every time she saw Fink of how she didn't measure up either.

Wishing she'd put on something a little fancier than the clothes she'd been working in, she nodded at Mrs. Herschel. "I see him."

"Oh good. Because there's my husband. I'm going to scoot on up to him. He's saved me a seat right beside him."

Which was more than Fink had done. He had the aristocratic woman on one side of him, and a woman with a small child on her lap on the other.

Mrs. Herschel dropped her hand from Ellie's arm. "I know he's expecting you. He said so, honey," she murmured, as though she'd sensed Ellie's hesitation.

She nodded. "Thanks, Mrs. Herschel."

"Go get him, Ellie dear." The little lady nodded at Fink. "He needs someone like you in his life."

Ellie smiled, like she assumed she was supposed to, and Mrs. Herschel climbed the bleacher steps.

Tempted to turn tail and run, Ellie glanced at the field before taking a deep breath and plunging through the students standing at the rail at the front of the bleachers. Cheerleaders chanted and danced in front of them as she wound her way through.

Most of the people in the stands were dressed like her—sweatshirts and jeans, minus the work boots—so Fink's group, in their dress coats, pressed slacks, and good shoes, stood out. She was only twenty feet away when he glanced up from his conversation with the woman holding the child, and his eyes met Ellie's. The serious expression melted away and a grin split his face. He stood, belatedly looking down and mouthing, "Excuse me," to the woman who had still been talking.

She waited while he scooted around the group he was with and strode toward her.

"Ellie! I'm sorry you walked over yourself. There's two minutes and forty-seven seconds left in the half. I was making myself wait until the two-minute mark to walk over." He grinned. "I didn't think you'd be early."

Okay. So he had a good point there. She did have a reputation for tardiness. She returned his smile, pleased that he'd acted a little like it'd been days, rather than hours, since he'd last seen her.

"Mrs. Herschel walked over with me." She shrugged. "I'm a big girl, though, really. I can be by myself."

"Well, I know your in-laws couldn't make it with you. I mean, I assumed they'd need to stay at the farm and keep things going."

"Yeah, they were disappointed that they couldn't come, but it's the sacrifice you make when you own a business." They had insisted that she go. She hadn't put up much of an argument.

"Come on over here and sit down. Do you mind?" he added as an afterthought.

"Not at all. Thanks for including me. This will be perfect to see Harper."

She almost thought he was going to take her hand, but he stuck his hand in his pocket instead, leading her to where he'd been sitting.

"Dr. Rothschild, this is Ellie Bright. Her daughter, Harper, is homecoming queen, and she's going to watch the ceremony with us."

Danielle's lips flattened as her cold blue eyes narrowed. Her gaze skimmed over Ellie's work attire.

"Ellie and I know each other," Danielle said coolly.

Fink's brows furrowed.

Ellie lifted her chin and held her hand out. "It's been a while, Danielle." She glanced at Fink. "Until I quit, we were in the same class in school."

Danielle used three fingers and touched Ellie's hand with light pressure. Her mauve fingernails glinted in the light. Her gaze, narrowed and calculating, slid to Fink before landing back on Ellie. "Congratulations on your daughter's election." If one could look down one's nose while looking up at a person, Danielle had accomplished it.

"Thanks." Ellie tried to sound sincere.

"Do you mind sliding over, and she and I will sit on the end?" Fink asked.

Danielle moved her posterior over, and Fink indicated for Ellie to sit beside her.

By the time Ellie got settled and looked up, only a few seconds were left in the half.

Fink leaned over to her ear. "I'm so glad you could make it. I think Harper is pretty excited."

"I bet she is. I've texted her, but it's Friday, which is always busy at the farm, and I haven't talked to her. She wasn't even set on going to the dance, since we're shorthanded, so we'll actually have to go shopping tomorrow for a dress." Ellie hadn't figured out how they were going to accomplish that. Saturdays were busy all day.

"Want me to come out in the morning for a while to help out?"

Her head spun around. She almost bumped his nose with hers, he was that close. "Would you?"

"Of course. I owe you." He lowered his voice. "These people really sound interested in our district, and the float you've made will only be an asset."

"Is there something special about these people?"

"They've got money." He shrugged.

"I see." The wind gusted and she reached up to tuck a strand of hair behind her ear. Fink captured her hand with his own. He kissed her knuckle before tucking their clasped hands into his jacket pocket.

Her eyes widened. "People might see."

"It's hard to care. You're so beautiful with your bright cheeks and flashing eyes. Natural. It's magnetic."

She couldn't believe Fink was holding her hand. He squeezed it, and they shared a smile before the loudspeaker crackled, announcing the royalty parade.

If someone had told her she'd be watching her daughter ride around the Chestnut Hill football field in the back of a pickup as homecoming queen, she might have believed it. If they had added that Ellie would be holding Mr. Finkenbinder's hand while she watched, she'd have laughed in their face. But she was. And it felt perfect.

After the announcements ended, the royalty were introduced, and the parade looped the track, the loudspeaker squawked with calls to support the Boosters by purchasing food at their stand, and people began getting up and walking around.

"I'd better get going," she said, but couldn't seem to get her butt to leave the seat.

"I'll walk you out."

"You don't need to."

"But I can, if I want to?"

"Of course."

He stood, letting go of her hand, but putting his on the small of her back after she stood. He faced Danielle. "Ellie has to go back to work. I'm walking her out. Would you like anything? A burger or fries or drink?"

"No thank you," Danielle said through pinched lips.

"She doesn't like me much," Ellie said, after they'd reached the bleacher steps and started down.

"She doesn't like me either, but she's the president of the school board, and I need her vote on Wednesday."

Ellie had gotten a different impression of Danielle's affections for Fink, but she kept her mouth shut.

A gangly teen rushed up the steps, tripping, and knocked into Ellie. She lost her balance and stumbled into Fink. He grabbed her to keep her from falling off the last two steps.

"Mr. Rheems. Watch yourself," he said to the teen.

"I'm sorry, Mr. F. Ma'am. Are you okay?" The kid's face was solid red and he shuffled his large feet.

"I'm fine." Ellie had caught her balance with no harm done, but Fink again had ahold of her hand. This time, their linked hands were not in his pocket.

"Be careful, Mr. Rheems, and don't run on the bleachers."

"Yes, sir, Mr. F." The boy turned and continued up the stairs. Slowly.

Fink looked down at Ellie. "Are you really okay? He hit you pretty hard."

"I'm fine. Really." She stared into his eyes, breathless, but not from getting bumped by a high school boy. It had more to do with Fink holding her hand in plain view of everyone.

"Let's go." He finished descending the stairs and their fingers stayed entwined.

After skirting the edge of the track, they started up the hill. Students and parents alike greeted Fink as they passed. More than one raised an eyebrow.

Figuring he must not realize they were still linked, she tried to pull her hand away. He tightened his fingers and looked down at her. He lifted their hands.

"This bothers you?"

"I thought you didn't realize. I don't mind at all."

"I realize." His hand squeezed hers. "Maybe you should mind. Because I wanted to take you behind the bleachers and do more than just hold your hand."

Her eyes popped open. "Fink?"

"How could anyone spend the week working with you and not fall under your spell?"

"Spell?"

He shook his head. "It must be a spell. I've been working toward the superintendent position for almost fifteen years, trying to shuck the farm boy from Iowa image. But right now, I don't care about that, or Dr. Rothschild, or the families thinking about choosing to relocate to our district. Any of it. I want to leave with you, be with you. I don't even recognize myself. That's some spell."

"I'm shocked."

His mouth tightened. It was much less crowded this close to the gate, but Fink was quiet as they passed a high school couple walking in, holding hands.

He turned, maybe to make sure the couple was out of earshot, before he walked through the gate with her. Then he pulled her over toward an equipment shed, out of the light.

"You could say, 'Fink, I feel the same about you,'" he said roughly.

"I thought you knew it."

"Aren't we having this conversation backward? Isn't it the woman who's supposed to say, 'I need to hear the words'? And the man who says, 'I told you once, and if anything changes I'll let you know'?"

She laughed, as maybe he intended. He pulled her hand, spinning her until her back was against the dark side of the shed. He moved closer, releasing her hand to wrap his around her waist, his other hand in her hair.

"I saw you leaving this morning, and my whole body ached to talk to you. Touch you. Actually, I had a whole group of people in my office and all I could think about was running after you and doing this." His mouth covered hers.

She kissed him back eagerly. Her arms went around his neck, pulling him closer.

He groaned.

She caught the sound in her mouth, savoring it. He wanted her. He'd thought about kissing her.

Holy cow, he *was* kissing her. Even with the passion that had erupted in her chest, she couldn't contain her giggle.

He lifted his head, his breathing choppy. His hand splayed flat on the shed wall beside her head. "My kissing is funny?"

"Gosh, no. Never. My head is spinning and I can't think, but I don't want you to stop."

"You laughed."

"I'm making out with the principal behind the equipment shed. It has a surreal quality to it."

"I see." His thumb traced down her cheek, along her jawline. "Surreal in a good way?"

His voice was tender, but a little uncertain. Her heart leaped in response. She pulled him closer, standing on tiptoe to kiss his hard jaw. "The best way."

He growled and his mouth came back down on hers. His hand slid over her T-shirt. She shivered and pushed closer. His fingers spanned her waist, but he pulled his head back and rested his forehead on hers.

"I was going to wait until Thursday. I didn't want anything to interfere with the decision for superintendent, but I spent the day thinking it didn't matter if I even got the position anymore. As principal, I have summers off and could help you on the farm. As superintendent that would be impossible." He took a deep breath. "That's making an awful big assumption that you want me to help."

"I want you." She pulled back. "But I don't want you to miss out on a career opportunity because of being seen with me." It hurt to say it. Hurt to think people might think less of him for being with her. But small-town folk had long memories. No one had forgotten she'd gotten pregnant at fifteen and never finished high school. Was that the type of person they wanted their school superintendent to marry? For the most part, probably not.

He held her chin and seemed to search her eyes in the darkness. "Didn't you hear me say I don't care?"

"But I do."

He huffed. "Are we still on the float tomorrow night?"

"Yes. Dad needs to be at the farm, so our neighbor is driving the tractor."

"As long as we're together behind the moon."

She laughed and cupped his cheek with her hand. "Please don't allow me to stand between you and the superintendent position."

"Please don't push me away just because I have a degree and a position in the school administration."

Ellie froze. That could be true. She might be just as bigoted as she'd been accusing him of being. "If I'm pushing you away, it's not because you have an education. It's because I don't."

"Isn't that the same as if I were to push you away because I do and you don't?" His fingers traced down her cheek.

"I expect that."

"Does that make it right?"

"It's normal."

"You're not judging me as a man, on my merits, but only on some slip of paper I have."

Her mouth opened and closed. "I'm sorry. I didn't realize, but that's exactly what I was doing." She leaned her head against the shed.

"A lot of times we're blind to our own prejudices. I know I was."

"Willfully blind." Had she been prejudiced? "Maybe when you think that other people are judging you, it's easier to judge them back rather than turn the other cheek."

"Maybe." He lowered his head and nuzzled her cheek.

She turned her head, meeting his lips. His hand moved on her waist, and she slid both her hands into his open jacket. He was solid muscle, and her fingers tingled as they learned his shape through his dress shirt.

He pressed closer and their kiss deepened.

She heard a moan, and she honestly wasn't sure if it was him or her.

"Mr. Finkenbinder?"

Ellie jerked back, recognizing the feminine voice.

Chapter Fourteen

D r. Rothschild stood at the edge of the shed, squinting into the darkness where they stood. Her low, sling-back pump tapped the gravel and she crossed her arms in front of her cream blouse and light blue dress coat. Her mouth was set in a straight, flat line.

"I don't think this is appropriate behavior. Not from the school principal, and certainly not from the district superintendent." Despite her civilized tone, her words were tight and clipped. Ellie closed her eyes. She'd thought the woman had a bit of a thing for Fink. Who wouldn't? And the adage about the fine line between love and hate seemed applicable here.

Unless Ellie moved to stop it, Fink's chances at superintendent were most likely gone.

"I'm sorry, Dr. Rothschild. Fink, um, Mr. Finkenbinder didn't know I was going to drag him behind the shed, and, uh, jump him."

"Well, that seems very believable to me, except for one thing." Dr. Rothschild tilted her head. "His hand is up your shirt."

"Well, you see, he was overcome—"

"Unlikely. You're not exactly a person who inspires a man to lose his head with lust."

"I beg to differ." Fink slid his hand out from under her sweatshirt. She closed her eyes from the sweet friction.

He caught her hand in his and moved toward Dr. Rothschild. "You might as well know that Ellie and I are dating. I am anxious and eager and hopeful she'll agree to something more permanent soon." He looked at Ellie with shining eyes. "Maybe by Christmas?"

Ellie didn't want to look like a dimwit in front of Dr. Rothschild, but she couldn't seem to get her mouth closed. She shook her head. "Permanent?"

"If you want me."

"Mr. Finkenbinder, I'm sorry, but the behavior you are currently displaying is still inappropriate. Whether you're dating or not. The actions of the administrator of a school must be above reproach at all times. If the families here find out that our principal was...engaged in a vulgar display of amorous attention behind the equipment shed... If they find out the woman you were kissing is a simple farmer who doesn't even have her high school diploma..."

That was harsh. And it hurt. But it was exactly what she'd been trying to tell Fink. That's how many of the people on the school board would see it. Sure, the community would probably rally around her, but Fink wouldn't get the job.

"You're right." Ellie broke away from Fink. "I really was pushing myself on him. But no one needs to know about this, unless you tell someone."

"I certainly will not."

"Ellie..." Fink touched her arm. "Please don't."

She jerked out of his reach. "No, Fink. I'm not spending the rest of my life being the chain around your neck. We need to stop this before we begin something we regret." She turned to Dr. Rothschild. "I give you my word that your superintendent will not be caught in any more vulgar displays with me, if you give me yours that the position is still his."

A small smile appeared briefly on Dr. Rothschild's face. "He is the most qualified candidate, and the most popular. He was also the most levelheaded. If you keep your word, the superintendent position is his."

"I'm out of the picture." She had to hold it together just a little bit longer. Calling on every last crumb of strength she had, she turned to Fink. "This is what you've worked for since you left Iowa. You'd better not screw it up." Tossing her head in a totally fake display of detachment, she strode away.

She did not allow herself to cry until she had pulled out of the parking lot.

~

FINK RUSHED from the game to Ellie's farm as fast as he could. It was possible he was slightly rude to Mrs. Cummings, the widow of the former oatmeal baron with two small children who, along with the Rosencrantzes, was considering the district. But the woman really needed to put her children to bed, and she wouldn't stop hanging on his arm.

Now, as he stepped out of his car, carrying the package containing Ellie's surprise, he wondered where the best place to look for her would be.

Spying Harper and Wyatt working at the campfire, he headed toward them.

"You both looked great tonight," he said as he stepped to the fire, stuffing the package under his arm and holding his hands out. There was a definite chill in the air tonight.

"Thanks, Mr. F." Harper handed a hot dog to a little girl whose mother stood behind her holding a stick. "Are you here to help?"

"Well, I was kind of looking for your mom, but I'm here to help too." He adjusted the package and glanced around.

"Gram and Pap are doing the haunted house, and Wyatt and I are splitting up between here and the pumpkin patch and apple bobbing, but no one's been giving hayrides all night. If you could do that, it'd be great."

"Where did you say your mom was?" She hadn't actually said where Ellie was, but Fink hoped she would with a little prompting.

"She said she had a headache and went in to lie down. It must be really bad because I can't remember her ever not working before."

"She looked awful," Wyatt said, his typical honest self.

Fink's heart thumped slowly and painfully. When she'd jerked away and dismissed him with such imperiousness, his whole world had tilted.

He'd never been immune to Ellie. Even his attempt to "punish" her for Harper's tardiness was calculated to get a reaction. Because he loved seeing her passion and her life. Because he loved her.

He tensed, stunned, as he allowed the thought to sink in. That knowledge was a shock, but he knew that it was true. The problem was, he wasn't sure how she felt.

She'd returned his kisses with passion and fervor, and she'd allowed him to hold her hand. He could almost believe she took the fall with Dr. Rothschild because she loved him and wanted the best for him. But he could be wrong. Maybe she wanted to continue to cling to her biases against his job and education. Perhaps Dr. Rothschild had reminded her that she'd believed the gap between them was too large. Or even Ellie might have decided she wasn't good enough. The thought broke his heart and made him angry because it wasn't true. Or she could have realized she didn't really like him.

She hadn't said. She hadn't done anything to make him think she might feel for him as he did her except return his embrace. Maybe she was simply lonely.

"Mr. F?" Harper waved her hand in front of his face. "Are you okay?"

"Yeah." He wanted to go to the house, storm in, and demand she answer him. But that was nuts. "I can drive the tractor."

The package in his hand crinkled as he moved, and he glanced at it. He'd forgotten about it.

"This is for the float. I'm going to stick it on the wagon, then I'll be back to start the hayrides."

"Thanks, Mr. F." Harper smiled as she handed out another hot dog.

He'd have to wait until tomorrow to talk to Ellie.

AFTER A SLEEPLESS NIGHT, Fink arrived at the farm at nine a.m. with a headache of his own. Not for the first time, he wished he drank coffee, but he couldn't abide the vile stuff. So he'd popped two painkillers before heading out.

Esther Bright, Ellie's mother-in-law, was in the shop.

"Good morning, Mr. Finkenbinder. How are you this beautiful fall day?"

Not as happy as she was, apparently. He hadn't noticed the day was beautiful. All he wanted was to see Ellie.

"Call me Fink, Mrs. Bright. I told Ellie I'd help out today."

"Oh, that's wonderful. Ellie never takes off. I hope they have a good time."

"Ellie isn't here?" His stomach fell. How could he talk to her, tell her how he felt, when she wasn't around?

"No. I thought that's why you were."

"I didn't know she wasn't going to be here." Frustration bubbled in his chest. Was she deliberately avoiding him?

"Harper has to go to the dance tonight and she didn't have a dress. They went to the city to go shopping. It's going to be busy today, and we'll miss them, but I'm glad they went. Ellie and Harper both spend too much time working. I can't remember the last time she took off, other than last night."

He pushed past his disappointment. "What do you want me to do?"

Esther began naming things that needed done. Fink listened with one ear while he got his phone out and texted Ellie.

Miss you.

By lunch time, he'd still not received a reply.

Are you mad at me?

He felt like a teenaged boy in a fight with his girlfriend. But he was desperate to talk to her.

Still no answer.

Shadows had begun to lengthen, but Ellie hadn't returned when Esther stopped by the fuel pump as he filled the tractor up. "We're closing early tonight, Mr. Finkenbinder."

"You are?" His brow furrowed. That was odd. Ellie had said weekend nights were the busiest for the farm.

"Yes. We are. We never do, even when it rains, but Harper is homecoming queen and that will only happen once in my lifetime. I didn't want Ellie to feel torn about being at the parade and going to the dance to see Harper crowned." She smiled sweetly. "Plus, I want to see it too."

"Oh, of course."

"So—" She glanced at her watch. "—it's almost five. We're turning people away. You can go on home and get ready."

"Is someone still driving the tractor for the float?" He hoped someone else was. Since he'd not seen Ellie all day, he was really looking forward to standing behind the moon with her.

"Our neighbor, Bob, is coming down at six. He'll have the float at the starting point in town by six fifteen or so."

"Great." The parade started at seven, then the dance at eight. It should be plenty of time. And, he thought as he pulled out of the farm parking lot, Ellie might have been able to avoid him all day, but she wouldn't be able to avoid him on the float.

UNLESS SHE DIDN'T SHOW up. Which is exactly what she did.

Fink stood beside the float, talking to a parent, when Harper, looking elegant in a long blue off-the-shoulder gown, and Wyatt, looking snazzy in his suit, which had been the first thing Fink had bought him when he came from Chile, because one never knew when a suit would come in handy, climbed up on the float.

Fink ended his current conversation abruptly. "Hey, guys," he said to Wyatt and Harper.

"Uncle Fink."

"Mr. F."

"Nice dress," Fink said to Harper, because he figured he should at least mention it before he interrogated her about Ellie.

"Thanks."

"Where's your mom?"

Esther shuffled over to him. "She's tired. She's not used to shopping all day. So she asked me if I would take her place with you."

"Where is she?" He checked his watch. Ten minutes until the parade started and they were the first float.

"She was at the farm when we left. She said she might come and watch if she felt up to it."

He tried not to growl, but was unsure if he was successful. She'd managed to avoid him all day.

"Did she say anything about me?" His pride lay in a heap at his feet, and he didn't even care.

"Mr. F?" Harper said from the float.

He looked up. "Yes?"

"Mom's being an idiot. I tried to tell her today. She insists you're too good for her and she'll just be an impediment to your career." She pursed her lips and looked as annoyed as he felt.

"Yeah, she said the same thing to me."

"So you don't agree?" Harper grinned.

"Of course not."

"Well, she said something about the school board president..." Harper raised her brows. "Apparently, it's more than just Mom's opinion."

"Dr. Rothschild is an idiot."

"But you need her vote."

"I don't give a hoot if she votes for me or not."

"Mom said she doesn't want to be the reason she, or anyone else on the board, doesn't vote for you."

"I can fix that." The words were out of his mouth before he thought about them. "I'm withdrawing my name from consideration."

Harper's brows rose. "Don't be rash, Mr. F."

"I'm not." And he realized it was true. He didn't actually want to be superintendent. He enjoyed working with the kids on a daily basis as principal. The administrative duties were just something he put up with. But as superintendent, that would be all he'd do.

Then why had he wanted the position in the first place?

The answer was obvious, but no longer relevant.

Chapter Fifteen

Ellie stood back in the crowd, anonymous, as the float chugged by.

Harper shone with an unmatched radiance as she and Wyatt waved to the cheering crowds lining the street. Ellie had a hard time believing that it was her daughter. She was so poised and beautiful. When had she grown up? It seemed like just yesterday that she'd brought a screaming infant home from the hospital, little more than a child herself, determined in her heart to figure out how to be both a mother and a wife. She hadn't been a very good wife—the kisses with Fink had shown her that. She'd never kissed Liam like she was starving and wanted to lose herself in him.

And mother? Well, Harper had pretty much become the kind and responsible person she was in spite of Ellie. Not because of her.

Her eyes went to the silhouettes in the moon. She had to smile. Mom held a pitchfork in one hand and wore an old straw hat on her head. And Fink. Her heart skipped and rattled in her chest. He stood with both feet planted, slightly apart, one hand on his hip, one resting on Esther's shoulder. A capable, masculine silhouette. Perfect.

The crowd murmured as the float drifted by. Pleased and excited and impressed, from what she could tell. Then she noticed the banner on the back.

HAVE YOU KISSED YOUR FARMER TODAY?

And beneath that appeared the name, address, and phone number of their farm in smaller lettering under the rhetorical question.

Fink didn't strike her as horribly romantic, but he'd come up with that—*Have you kissed your farmer today?*—himself. He certainly hadn't had help from her.

Tears pricked her eyes. Fink hadn't kissed his farmer today. She'd successfully avoided him all day. Plus, she wasn't his. Which was her own stupid fault. If only she could turn back time. Like eighteen years of time. But she wouldn't have Harper. And Harper was the best thing that had ever happened to her.

The float turned the corner and disappeared out of sight. Ellie slipped back through the crowd and got in her pickup. As principal, Fink would be at the dance. She hadn't quite figured out how to avoid him there, but she was determined to see Harper crowned. She'd even bought a dress for the occasion. Nothing fancy. This wasn't her night, after all. But nice enough. She hoped.

She pulled into the farm and parked the pickup in front of the house, then walked slowly up the dark path to the porch. Usually someone left the porch light on, but the house was dark. Even the harvest moon was hidden behind thick clouds.

The night air felt cool against her warm cheeks. Breathing in deeply, she savored the rich fall smells of corn tassels, black soil, tangy leaves, and a trace of woodsmoke. It wasn't usually this quiet here, and she soaked in the peaceful isolation. A soft breeze lifted her hair from where it lay in some semblance of order, thanks to industrial-strength hair gel, on her neck.

She was making the right decision about Fink—letting him go—but her heart felt empty.

Funny that they'd only spent this week together, but somehow he seemed a part of her life. One it was hurtful to remove.

She adjusted her purse strap over her shoulder and moved toward the porch steps, feeling for the railing in the dark.

With Harper graduating, she wouldn't even have an excuse to see Fink anymore. Not that he'd be around anyway. The superintendent had his own set of offices in the back of the elementary school. She'd never even seen them, although they were probably nice. Plush. Real wood furniture rather than the plastic-veneered stuff Fink had in his office right now. He deserved better. Better furniture. A better woman.

"Hey."

She jumped, then froze. "Fink?"

"Yeah. It's me," he said softly.

"But you were on the float." How did he beat her here? The parade wasn't even over when she left.

"Jordon did it for me."

"Oh." Of course.

"I got the impression you were avoiding me."

"You got it right. Smart one." Sarcasm was one of her walls. She felt safer hiding behind it.

"Why?"

"I told you yesterday, I'm not starting something with you that we're going to regret."

"You'll regret."

"You. I'm not on the level that you need."

He sighed, barely audible. "Do you have a minute?"

"I need to go in and get ready to go to the dance." She couldn't spend any more time with him. The longer she spent with him, the deeper she fell.

"Sit down." He said it in his principal's voice, and she had obeyed before she even thought not to.

"I told you I grew up on a farm in Iowa."

"Yeah." She picked at her purse strap. Not that she could see it in the dark.

"I left the farm as soon as I could."

"I know."

"I didn't tell you why."

"You went to college." She knew that.

"Dad wanted me to take over the farm. Be a farmer. There's pride in working with your hands, he'd say."

"I agree." She had a feeling she would have liked his dad.

"Well, I didn't. I was ashamed of my working-class roots. My country-bumpkin background. My rural ignorance. I admired the culture and class of the urbanites. You know they look down on country folk? Some of them, anyway. Some of them—like me."

That hurt. But she'd figured he'd looked down on her. She hid the pain with a question, unable to keep the accusing tone out of her voice. "What are you doing at a little school like this? You like the city so much, go live in the city."

"I did. For a while. But I hated it. The noise and the crowds, the filth and the feeling of isolation even in the midst of piles of people. So proud that we're big and inclusive, but you can't get a single person to even look you in the eye on the sidewalk, yet alone to say hi to a stranger."

Well, that was different. "Heck, we wave to everybody around here."

"I know. People have actually stopped at the school and stormed into my office, just to ream me out for not waving to them, and I don't even know where they saw me. Just easier to wave to everyone." He laughed softly to himself. "Remember when I said that sometimes we're particularly blind to our own biases?"

"Yeah."

"It's true for urbanites as well as us." He shifted. "Anyway, I hated the city life, but I didn't want the Iowa farm-boy label either. So when a teaching position at Chestnut Hill came up, I jumped. I love it here. I drive by the farms, maybe a little smaller than my childhood—and we didn't have these hills and mountains. But it feels like home. Because the people are the same. Friendly. Hardworking. Stuck in their ways, but willing to help anyone out."

"Fink, I really don't understand why you're telling me all this."

"Just listen." A note of irritation crept into his tone. Softer, he said, "Please?"

She allowed her silence to be her answer.

After a few moments he went on. "I loved the rural school district, but I kept after my education too. There's more than one kind of bias. I might live in the country, but I was an academic. White collar. I taught, then was the administrator for, the blue collars. And, of course, during all of that, my mom died and my dad asked me to come home."

"But you didn't."

"I wasn't ready. Much as I missed the farm, I still wasn't ready to admit there was no difference in value between an educated elite and an ignorant country bumpkin."

"No difference in value?"

"No. Sometimes we think that because we have a degree, it makes us better."

"It takes work to get a degree. That shows diligence and perseverance."

"And it takes work to make a farm successful. A marriage successful. To raise a child who is homecoming queen and valedictorian. That, too, takes perseverance and diligence."

Ellie didn't say anything. She hadn't really thought about it, but she supposed he was right.

"One isn't more valuable, or better, than the other. Much as I, or you, might want to think."

"I'm not disagreeing with you."

"I called Dr. Rothschild today."

Okay. Subject change, apparently. She shrugged. "So?"

"I told her I was no longer interested in the superintendent position. To take my name out of the hat."

She shoved to her feet and turned, even though she couldn't see him, planting her hands firmly on her hips. "You didn't."

"I never wanted the position. I wanted the prestige that went along with it. I wanted to bury that Iowa farmboy so deep, he'd never come up."

The stairs creaked, then he was in front of her, holding her shoulders, slipping his hands around her, and there was no strength in her to pull away.

"But that Iowa farm boy is a part of me. I'll always regret not going back home and taking over the farm. And if I allow you to think you're not good enough for me, if I let you think I want a job or prestige more than I want to be with you, I'll always regret that too. This week has opened my eyes in a lot of ways. I realized all that time, I actually enjoyed waiting for you to come rolling in, in your pickup. I admired your sass and your verve. I looked forward to seeing you. Every day. I think I fell in love with you long before you sat down in my office last Monday—it doesn't really matter when. I love you now."

Her heart beat crazily in her chest, and her mouth opened and closed, but she couldn't force out any words. The night air, the peek-a-boo moon, the softly scented breeze on her cheeks—it all felt like a dream. But Fink was solid and warm in front of her, his hands tender on her shoulders, and his voice floated on the night air.

"If you don't love me for who I am, that will be hard, but okay. But if you reject me because of what I do, or because of some piece of paper that's attached to my name, I'm going to fight you. Because I love you. And I want to be with you. And I'm willing to fight for that." He stopped talking and held her against him.

She felt like the whole world was spinning and she gripped him tightly. She could hardly believe it was true. That Fink had just said he wanted to be with her. That he would fight for her.

Her stomach clenched, and she put a hand on it as she thought of Izzy in the pumpkin patch and the fear that kept her from choosing a pumpkin. The same fear that threatened now to keep Ellie from reaching out for her own pumpkin. Fear of change. Fear of loving and losing again. Fear of not measuring up to Fink's high standards or the standards the community might have for the principal's wife. Fear that Fink might resent her eventually.

The excitement that Fink loved her threatened to be overwhelmed by those fears. But she could she face them. She could step out, away from her comfortable life, and risk losing everything again. Risk facing her insecurities, believing that love could conquer all. She squared her shoulders and took a deep breath. Because of Fink, because of the man he was, she could do this.

The crickets and occasional rustle of the wind in the leaves were the only sounds. "Say something, Ellie."

"Don't quit."

He laughed. A strangled sound. "Don't quit what? Talking? My job?"

"Either. Both." She took a breath, feeling like she was stepping off a cliff. "I love you, too, Fink."

"Ellie," he breathed, before he lowered his head and kissed her. She returned the embrace with all the tangled emotions inside.

He pulled back, and his breath came in short gasps. "Does this mean you're willing to take a chance on me? Or does it just mean I won the first skirmish?"

She snuggled into his warmth. "I probably shouldn't admit this, but I like fighting with you."

He groaned. "I kind of like fighting with you too. Well, maybe it's the making up that I most enjoy."

She snorted.

Fink leaned back and seemed to search her face in the shadows. "Anything else. We can fight about anything else. But I need to know we're together in this. You and me."

"You better be careful. Once I'm stuck, it's pretty hard to get rid of me."

"I don't want rid of you." He nuzzled her neck, and she closed her eyes and leaned her head back. "Think your in-laws will be okay with us?"

She tried to focus. "I think. If not, I love them, but I'll leave. I've been as true to Liam as I could be." She ran her hands down his back. "I think they want me to be happy. In order for me to be happy, I need to be with you."

"I need to show up at this dance tonight, much as I'd rather stay here. Do you think you might consider coming as my date?" Again, that little note of insecurity lightly shaded his question.

"Chaperones can have dates?"

"The teachers usually bring their spouses. I've never taken anyone."

She liked that. As far as she knew, Fink had been so focused on his career, she'd never heard of him dating. Happiness bloomed in her chest. "I was going to see Harper crowned anyway. I bought a dress."

"Mmm. Need help getting it on?" His breath brushed her ear.

"Mr. Finkenbinder. I'm shocked."

"That was a yes."

"That was a 'you wait right here, I'll be back out in a few minutes,'" she said with mock huffiness.

"What do I have to do to be able to help?" His hand stroked down her back.

She shivered. "I'm a country girl with small-town values. A man needs a legal right to be in my bedroom."

"Sounds like I need to make a stop at the jewelry store."

"That'd be the first step."

The clouds parted and the full autumn moon in all its brightness shone down. Fink whispered in her ear, "Have you kissed your farmer today?"

"I did."

"No, that was him kissing you."

She smiled up at him. He'd just called himself a farmer. His parents were probably smiling right now. "Then I guess I haven't."

"Maybe you'd better get on that, Mrs. Bright."

"I love you, Fink." She put her arms around her farmer. And kissed him.

Join Jessie's list and be the first to know about new releases and sales on her books!

Read Better Together, the next book in the Sweet Haven Farm series. Harper and Wyatt's story! Love kindles when a fake engagement brings best friends together. Keep reading for a sneak peek now.

Sneak Peek of Better Together

"No way am I going in there." Harper Bright took a second look at the yawning black hole in the mountain in front of her and crossed her arms over her chest. She didn't need her doctorate degree to know this was a bad idea.

"Did you know this tunnel was on Hitler's charts during World War II? If he ever made it stateside, it was one of the places he planned to bomb." Wyatt Fernandez planted his feet and put his hands on his hips. His dimples flashed but he spoke in the tone of voice that said, "I hear you, but I'm ignoring you".

He used the same tone every time he dragged Harper on some crazy adventure or another.

She walked toward the openmouthed hole. Despite her family having owned the ground around the tunnel all her life, she hadn't known about this small spot in Central Pennsylvania being on Hitler's map.

The looming mountain that shot up around the ravenous cavity blocked the sunlight. Leafy green trees waved in the warm June breeze. Harper squinted up. "You know, someday, we really ought to start acting like the mature adults we are."

"Gimme a break, Harper. The only time you ever spend two

seconds not acting like an adult is when I strong arm you into it. Like now. This is going to be fun." Wyatt flashed that irresistible dimple and his brown eyes twinkled. Harper wasn't exactly short, but she still had to crane her neck to look at him as he walked beside her. His lanky frame had filled out in the decade since high school. Actually, now that she thought about it, he'd filled out very nicely. Broad chest, wide shoulders, and long, muscular legs. A flare of heat unfurled in her stomach. She straightened her spine. This was Wyatt. Her best friend.

They reached the orifice of the mountain. Cool air blew from its depths. It smelled heavy and sweet, like rotting soil. Their next steps took them inside. The hair on the back of Harper's neck poked straight out. She scooted closer to Wyatt.

"I'm not seeing the 'fun' part." Her voice echoed off the cavernous walls. Water dripped hollowly, echoing in the blackness.

Wyatt kept walking. "This isn't supposed to be fun. It's research. Do you want to find it or not?"

Harper bumped Wyatt's arm with her shoulder. "You know I do."

She wanted to see if the old stories were true, but couldn't help shivering as she looked around at the stone walls arching above. The farther in they walked, the darker it got. At this point, she could barely see Wyatt's outline. She pushed back the fear threatening to break loose in her head. It wasn't that walking in the tunnel was particularly dangerous. It was more the idea of the dark unknown and being trapped in a small space with an angry locomotive.

As if Wyatt could read her mind, he said, "There isn't any danger if a train would actually go through while we're in here. Although, I have heard that there could be a bit of air suction."

She planted her feet. "What?"

"Kidding." He pulled on her arm. "Come on."

She started walking again. Slowly. "What did you mean by air suction?" Wyatt had always been better with hard science. All she'd cared about was finding the family heirloom that her great-great grandmother had told her was hidden in the deepest depths.

Wyatt tapped her head with the hand that wasn't dragging her toward the tunnel. "Well, since you're the brain in this relationship..."

She swatted his hand and continued to drag her feet, even though she'd already decided to go along with his nutty scheme, the way she always did. After all, not only did she want to find the ring, but this could be the last time Wyatt and she went on an adventure together. She'd gotten the call yesterday that her tenure vote was scheduled for the end of summer. It was the one last thing she had to cross off the list of career goals she'd made the day she had graduated from high school.

"Quit it. You're smarter than me, and we both know it. I just happen to be able to stay in one place long enough to get a degree." It wasn't that she was so smart. She was simply willing to work hard. Plus, she liked to study. She'd enjoyed every second of the last ten years. Which led her to the vexatious question that had plagued her since the phone call: *what now?*

"Ouch." Wyatt placed a hand over his heart.

She shrugged. Too often she'd wondered that maybe what she'd been working toward all this time wasn't what she really wanted anymore. More likely she had become overly comfortable with achieving her goals, ticking each accomplishment off of her internal checklist. "It's true."

"Yeah, well, you had a nice, secure home all your life."

And he hadn't. Never really knowing or being wanted by his father, losing his mother in a tragic skiing accident, being sent to live with an uncle he barely knew. Of course, if he hadn't come to live with the man her mother eventually married, she would never have gotten to know him. She bit her lip. "I'm sorry."

"Hey, not a problem. I'll only rub it in if you change your mind and turn around."

They walked far enough into the tunnel that the light behind them faded, and Harper could no longer see the road under her feet. Dread balled and rolled in the pit of her stomach. She reached for Wyatt. Big and strong with rough calluses, his hand enfolded hers with an ease born of familiarity.

How could she have forgotten how easily Wyatt's touch could calm her? All the numerous phone conversations and thousands of text messages couldn't replicate the comfort of his touch. The miles between them had always multiplied Harper's anxiety. The pictures he sent hadn't helped. Standing at the top of some snow-covered mountain with only clouds and sky in the background, or his arms outstretched, moments before he leapt from a who-knows-how-high cliff with only a thin bundle—hopefully a parachute—strapped to his back. Of course, she wasn't sure which was worse, the pictures, or the times when she didn't hear from him for days. He always warned her when he might be adventuring out of service areas, but that was one instance when knowledge wasn't power, as her ragged, bloody nails could testify.

"Do you think we're halfway?" she asked.

"Why are you whispering?"

She shivered—she hadn't noticed she was whispering. "Just in case there's a bear hibernating in one of those alcoves you talked about."

"It's June."

"Maybe it's waking up late this year." Even to her ears it sounded asinine. Her cheeks heated. She looked over, but they were so deep in the mountain that she couldn't see a thing. The darkness hid her flush. Lifting her chin, she tried to focus on the stories she'd heard as a child. If they found what they were looking for, it would be worth facing her fear.

"I can't believe someone has actually hired you to teach college students." He squeezed her hand, and she didn't need a light to know he smiled beside her.

"I revert to my inner child when I'm scared spitless."

Wyatt activated his cell phone light. "There." He pointed it at the wall. Sure enough, just ahead an arched area was chiseled into the side of the mountain. "Maybe three feet deep, three feet long and," he looked up, "seven or so feet high. We'd both fit in there easy."

"Us and the serial killer that eludes the cops by hiding in here." She tugged on his hand. "Come on. Faster."

"Didn't you ever hear you gotta enjoy the journey?" Harper could hear the grin in Wyatt's voice, but he did speed up a notch. For her. Heck, this was child's play compared to the stuff he normally did.

But it was Wyatt, and she didn't have to pretend to be brave. "I'll enjoy it once we're out of here."

"It'll be over then." He chuckled. "Oh, except we have to walk back through."

She stopped so fast her feet probably left skid marks. But she wouldn't know since it was darker than sin, and she couldn't see a blasted thing except for the far tunnel opening which didn't seem to be getting any closer.

"We only have to go to the middle hidey hole. That's where it's supposed to be. No one said anything about walking through." Fear had turned her backbone into an icicle. "I know you're an adrenaline junkie, but I'm allergic to the stuff."

Wyatt snorted. "If it weren't for me, you'd be moldering under your books and lab rats. How many times have you left the state?"

"Three. And it was three too many. I like being home. I like moldering." She kept her eyes fastened to the circle of light on the ground from Wyatt's cell phone until he put it away.

"I like being home, too. But being home is sweeter after you've left it for a while." His thumb moved lightly over her knuckles.

A little of her tension eased. "I always assumed you had itchy feet like your mom."

"A little, I guess."

"If that's not it, why not come home? You know Fink and my mom would love to have you back helping out on the farm." She'd love to have him back, too. Gosh, she missed him. She hadn't realized how much.

Even though he'd been away more than home the last few years, she still considered him her best friend. They had always told each other everything.

Well, except anything that even hinted of romance. Growing up, she'd always been very aware that her mother had gotten pregnant with her at fourteen. Harper had determined not to go down the same path, closing herself off to the very idea of boys or boyfriends. Studying instead of dating. She supposed, at twenty-eight, it was probably okay to crack that protective shell.

"Come on, Pickles. We're almost half-way. The next hidey-hole is probably close." His deep voice rumbled above her.

She smiled at the nickname he had gifted her with years ago.

Light cut through the darkness parallel to the ground—the wrong angle for Wyatt's cell phone—just before he tensed beside her. The rumble in the air and the vibration under her feet confirmed what her brain had suspected. She turned to be sure. The entire mouth of the tunnel was blocked out by the massive shape of a train engine. Like a flesh-eating bacteria, magnified, with teeth bared, it bore down on them.

Acid shards cut through her trembling body. She barely felt Wyatt yanking on her arm. She couldn't get her feet to move. The engine powered closer like a black avalanche, chewing up the distance between them.

He swept her up in his arms and jogged the two steps to the nook, flattening himself against the side wall so his back was toward the train. The roar of the engine and the squeal of metal on steel reverberated throughout the stone walls. The vibration seemed to be alive, monstrous, so close and big and loud she could almost see it. She pulled her body into a ball and pressed against him. She wrapped her arms around his head, wanting to protect him, too.

Her breath came in short gasps. Panic rolled through her like a bowling ball heading toward the king pin.

She closed her eyes tight, until it was only Wyatt's solid, comforting warmth pressing into her and the deafening noise all around. He cradled her and bent over slightly. The tangy, heavy stench of diesel exhaust filled the air around them, burning Harper's nose.

Eventually the engine noise faded away and, although the train was still loud, the cars passing had a more rhythmic feel. Loud clack-clack, then fading out before coming back combined with the occasional earsplitting screech of metal on metal.

Wyatt's stubble rubbed her cheek. She closed her eyes and moved her cheek back over his. Her chest tingled. She froze and her eyes snapped open. This was Wyatt. Her best friend. She would not allow their friendship to be ruined because she all of a sudden had some wild ribbon of desire winding through her. No matter how delicious it was.

His breath warmed her ear as he said, "Now we know there's no air suction."

"I'm going to poison the next meal I make you," she hissed into his neck, only half-joking.

"I've heard that before." His heart beat steady and strong against her. The dratted man wasn't even scared.

The last of the cars went by. The noise faded.

She loosened her arms from around his head. She didn't know what she was trying to protect him from anyway.

It was probably time to remember she was a grown-up. A professor up for tenure vote at the end of the summer. But Wyatt's warmth and strength were alluring. She didn't want to pull away from the hardness of his chest or lose the comfort of his touch. But she couldn't let him stand here holding her forever.

"Okay, put me down." She lifted her head and smacked his shoulder lightly, pretending she hadn't been clutching him like two oxygen atoms on a hydrogen, and praying her knees wouldn't buckle when he complied.

She wiggled to prompt him to move, but a new sound echoed in the darkness and she froze. A hiss. Followed by a rattle.

"Holy crap." Her arms tightened around Wyatt's neck. "Is that what I think it is?"

"Yeah. Someone's practicing the maracas." She could feel his head tilt in the darkness. "They're pretty good."

Her teeth rattled together, but she snorted a laugh. "That's a rattlesnake. It sounds close."

"I don't think we need to worry. I thought it was a stick when I first stepped on it, but sticks don't typically wrap themselves around your leg."

Chills raced up Harper's spine. Her mouth opened, but it took a minute to make her voice work. "You're standing on the snake?"

"Yes, ma'am."

The sound like stones shaking in a tin can echoed throughout the tunnel again.

She ignored the note of sarcasm in his voice. "What are we going to do?"

"You're the one with the doctorate. How about I keep standing on the snake while you think?"

Her throat slammed shut. She struggled to swallow. "I study nutrition. In a lab. That's what the doctorate is for. Food."

"Branch out a little."

Despite Harper's all-encompassing fear, she smiled. "Okay." She took a deep breath. If he wasn't worried, if he thought it was funny, well, she could do humor, too. "I'm thinking about white sandy beaches, relaxing waves, warm sun…"

"Try again."

She grinned—still petrified, but Wyatt exuded calm. "Hey, that was helping."

He snorted.

Ideas were not exactly filling her mind. Her brain had diverted all her blood flow to the areas that made her want to pee and run at the same time. She went with the only plan she could think of. "How about I grab your cell phone out of your pocket. I'll shine the flashlight down at your feet…"

"Um, close your eyes while you do it, just in case…"

Harper twisted gingerly in his arms and felt for the phone attached to his belt, not wanting to make him lose his balance, although he seemed rock solid. Funny, because she still pictured Wyatt as a gangly teen instead of the unflappable man holding her in his arms and not even breathing hard. "Just in case what?"

Silence.

"Wyatt. Is there something you're not telling me?"

"Not really."

Not really? That meant there was something. What could be worse than a rattlesnake? "If there was a bear in this hidey hole, I'd have figured it out by now."

"I'm sure you would have, Pickles." He shifted ever so slightly. "Would you just shine the light down?"

She paused with the phone in her shaking hand. "What does 'not really' mean? You're standing on the snake, right?"

"One of them."

"Holy crap. Holy crap. Holy crap."

He gave her the password to his phone. She pulled up the flashlight app with shaking fingers. Something caught her eye in a crack in the stone behind Wyatt's head. Her racing heart jumped. She squinted to see more clearly. She'd forgotten the reason they were in the tunnel in the first place.

"Harper? Tell me you're not playing Candy Crush."

"Uh. No. Of course not." She juggled the phone to her other hand.

Once they got the snake figured out, she could examine the crack more closely. There was definitely something there. Faded blue fabric, maybe?

She shone the light at the ground, keeping her eyes trained on the wall. Now that she knew something was there, she could see the shadow that marked the spot.

Wyatt shuddered. "Eh, I was wrong."

"Thank God." Cool relief flooded her. Her fingers lifted and skimmed the smooth surface of the stone.

"There's three."

She tensed.

Then yelped.

She dropped his phone.

Wyatt jerked.

With her free hand, she slapped at the wall. A small object landed in her palm.

Sign up for Jessie's newsletter! Get a free book, access to exclusive bonus content, get fun and funny updates on her life on the farm and more!

A Gift from Jessie

View this code through your smart phone camera to be taken to a page where you can download a FREE ebook when you sign up to get updates from Jessie Gussman! Find out why people say, "Jessie's is the only newsletter I open and read" and "You make my day brighter. Love, love, love reading your newsletters. I don't know where you find time to write books. You are so busy living life. A true blessing." and "I know from now on that I can't be drinking my morning coffee while reading your newsletter – I laughed so hard I sprayed it out all over the table!"

Claim your free book from Jessie!